20p
D0800078
WITHDRAWN
993143990 4

SPECIAL MESSAGE TO READERS

This book is published under the auspices of

THE ULVERSCROFT FOUNDATION

(registered charity No. 264873 UK)

Established in 1972 to provide funds for research, diagnosis and treatment of eye diseases. Examples of contributions made are: —

A Children's Assessment Unit at Moorfield's Hospital, London.

•

Twin operating theatres at the Western Ophthalmic Hospital, London.

•

A Chair of Ophthalmology at the Royal Australian College of Ophthalmologists.

•

The Ulverscroft Children's Eye Unit at the Great Ormond Street Hospital For Sick Children, London.

You can help further the work of the Foundation by making a donation or leaving a legacy. Every contribution, no matter how small, is received with gratitude. Please write for details to:

THE ULVERSCROFT FOUNDATION,
The Green, Bradgate Road, Anstey,
Leicester LE7 7FU, England.
Telephone: (0116) 236 4325

In Australia write to:
THE ULVERSCROFT FOUNDATION,
c/o The Royal Australian and New Zealand College of Ophthalmologists,
94-98 Chalmers Street, Surry Hills,
N.S.W. 2010, Australia

MARRIED TO THE ENEMY

Faced with the choice of death or marriage to a stranger, Kate marries Lord Alvedon, the powerful servant of Queen Elizabeth. Taken away from everything she has ever known Kate finds it difficult to adjust to the strange new world of Elizabeth's court. Her innocence not only threatens her marriage, it puts her in great danger — and, unknown to her or her husband, a secret enemy plans to kill both of them . . .

Books by Sheila Holroyd
in the Linford Romance Library:

ALL FOR LOVE
THE FACE IN THE MIRROR
DISTANT LOVE
FLIGHT TO FREEDOM
FALSE ENCHANTMENT
RELUCTANT LOVE
GREEK ADVENTURE
IN SEARCH OF THE TRUTH
ON TRIAL
ISLAND INTRIGUE
PURITAN BRIDE
KEEP ME FROM HARM
FAITHFUL TO A DREAM
A BAD BEGINNING
STAY WITH ME
HOME NO MORE
A HEART DIVIDED

SHEILA HOLROYD

MARRIED TO THE ENEMY

Complete and Unabridged

LINFORD
Leicester

Gloucestershire County
Council Library

British Library CIP Data

Holroyd, Sheila.
Married to the enemy - -
(Linford romance library)
1. Great Britain- -History- -Elizabeth I,
1558 – 1603- -Fiction. 2. Love stories.
3. Large type books.
I. Title II. Series
823.9′2–dc22

ISBN 978–1–84782–678–7

Published by
F. A. Thorpe (Publishing)
Anstey, Leicestershire

Set by Words & Graphics Ltd.
Anstey, Leicestershire
Printed and bound in Great Britain by
T. J. International Ltd., Padstow, Cornwall

This book is printed on acid-free paper

1

'Marry me, or die.' Kate stood silent and unmoving. The tall man shrugged impatiently. 'Surely it's a simple choice. Do you want to die?'

She shook her head mutely.

'Then I'll find a minister and make the necessary arrangements.'

He made a token bow and then swung on his heel, anxious to be gone. One problem had been solved but he had many others to deal with. Kate caught a glimpse of the armed guards stationed outside her door before he closed it firmly and she was free to feel for a chair and sink into it.

'Madam!' Jean, her young maid, was kneeling beside her, grasping her sleeve. 'Are you really going to marry him? What will happen to me?'

Kate managed a shuddering breath and found her voice. 'It does indeed look as if Lord Alvedon intends to marry me, but you must not worry, Jean. I'll still need you with me as my maid.'

The reassurance was not enough. Like Kate, the girl was finding it difficult to grasp how her life had changed so suddenly and she was on the edge of tears. She needed to be distracted so that Kate had time to think.

'Presumably Lord Alvedon will be taking us south with him soon. Look through my clothes and start to pack what you think we should take and put away what we can leave behind.'

Obediently the girl bustled off into the bedchamber, glad to be doing something which seemed to have some purpose, while Kate leant back gratefully and closed her eyes.

Twenty-four hours ago she had been waiting for her father and his followers to return from one of their raids across the Scottish border. The sixteenth century had drawn to a close, and the long reign of Queen Elizabeth of England would inevitably end soon. In Scotland King James waited impatiently to succeed her while the gentlemen of the Borders took advantage of the uncertain times to steal each other's cattle and pursue family feuds, sure that their rulers had more important things to do than try to control their petty activities.

Sir Harry Salter had summoned his men to ride with him more out of boredom than the need for a few cattle to feed them. He had laughed when Kate had protested that he was taking unnecessary risks.

'Don't worry, daughter. We'll show the Scots how easily we can take their stock and with a little luck we might enjoy a brisk fight with a few.'

'Suppose this time you don't come home safely? Think about me!'

He tipped up her chin with one finger and smiled down at her.

'Don't ill-wish me, Kate. Anyhow, if something happens to me I'm sure you will manage. You are a very capable young woman.'

As he rode away she waved after her light-hearted, charming, but not altogether reliable father. He had always returned safely before and of course he would this time, she told herself. But as evening fell a handful of his men appeared, riding for the safety of the castle as fast as their tired horses would carry them.

'We were on our way back,' one of them told Kate. 'We had a few cattle and we'd driven off the Scots after a short skirmish so there didn't seem to be any danger. Then suddenly we found ourselves facing horsemen — trained soldiers. Apparently they belonged to some English nobleman who was returning from an errand from Queen Elizabeth to King James. The men whose cattle we had taken had complained to him about us and he had decided to show the Scots that he was ready to enforce the English law.'

'Where's my father?' Kate demanded.

The man shrugged uncertainly. 'We couldn't face trained and heavily armed troops, so we scattered. Sir Harry said it was each man for himself, and that we should make our way back here somehow. I don't know what happened to him after we parted.'

'Will the troops come here?'

He avoided her eyes. 'It's possible.'

Kate ordered the castle gates to be shut and men posted on the walls, but the early morning light showed very few defenders. Too many men had quietly slipped over the walls during the night and made their way home to families who would swear they had not been out of their sight for a week.

At ten in the morning a body of well-armed horsemen was seen approaching the castle. They halted safely out of pistol-range and one of them advanced under a white flag. Kate ordered that he should be admitted by the postern gate to where she stood to receive him in the castle courtyard. He looked a little disconcerted when he found himself facing a woman.

'In the absence of my father, Sir Harry Salter, I am in charge here,' she told him. 'You may tell me your errand.'

The burly soldier took his time before he answered, glancing round with contempt at the handful of men visible.

'Your father, Sir Harry Salter, together with a band of his followers, was found stealing cattle yesterday. He and his men are thieves, and will be treated as such. The Earl of Mayburn, on behalf of Her Majesty Queen Elizabeth, calls upon you in the absence of your father to surrender this castle.'

Kate squared her shoulders as if physically aware of her responsibility, and the messenger continued, 'Lord Alvedon, the Earl of Mayburn, calls on you and your men to surrender to him, so that the law may be brought to bear on the cattle thieves.'

Kate was aware of the tension that suddenly filled the courtyard when the few defenders heard who was leading the attackers. Philip Alvedon, Earl of Mayburn, had inherited vast wealth at a young age from his father, who had been one of Queen Elizabeth's most devoted and trusted advisors. Now it was said that the Queen relied on the son even more than she had on the father. He was said to be intelligent and ruthless, as well as an experienced soldier. They were facing a formidable opponent.

Kate drew herself up. 'I have only to order the gates shut and we will be safe in the castle. Why should I surrender?'

'Because if you don't, we will either starve you out, or send for cannons and blast you out.'

It was concise, it was brutal, and Kate knew she had no answer. All she could do was try to mitigate the harm. It gave her some small satisfaction to make the messenger wait in the courtyard while she carefully composed a document in which she stated that she would surrender the castle in return for an amnesty for any 'suspected' cattle thieves found in the castle, together with an assurance that there would be no looting and that no violence would be done to any of her retainers.

It was unlikely that these terms would be agreed to, especially the first, but the debate would give her time to think and her men time to escape. The messenger took her document, telling her that the Earl himself was not yet with his soldiers outside the castle but would arrive soon.

An hour later she could see a stir as another group of horsemen joined the troops, and after an agonising wait the messenger returned and told her, to her considerable surprise, that the Earl had agreed to her conditions. It was much later before she realised that the Earl saw his encounter with Sir Harry as a mere irritating accident distracting him from the Queen's errand, and that he had no wish to waste time on pursuing and hanging a few cattle thieves. He had shown the Scots he would uphold the law. That was sufficient.

The castle gate was opened and its few remaining defenders laid down their arms and were shepherded into the hall and put under guard. Kate, waiting in her private apartments to receive the Earl of Mayburn, saw from her window half-a-dozen men ride into the courtyard and dismount. Minutes later there was a knock on the door and the guards outside threw it open without bothering to enquire her wishes, and she was face to face with her conqueror.

Philip Alvedon was about thirty years old, tall, and his hair was nearly as dark as her own. Most women would have thought him handsome, but there was a coldness about his expression which robbed him of attractiveness. Under his leather jerkin he wore a sober suit of black broadcloth with a white linen collar trimmed discreetly with a little lace. There was no need for him to wear rich armour or clothes to proclaim his leadership. He was a man accustomed to power, and it showed in the way he regarded the rest of the world.

Looking at Kate, he saw a tall girl whose slenderness was disguised by her full-skirted dress and whose black hair was drawn back from a white face stained with shadows under her dark eyes. With no touch of lace or ornament to relieve her mourning black, she was drained of colour, trying to look proud and defiant in a vain attempt to conceal the fear she felt.

He looked at her without saying a word till the colour rose in her cheeks and she held out the keys to the castle as a sign of formal surrender. As he took them from her, bowing formally and handing them to a guard, she spoke urgently.

'Lord Alvedon, I do not know what has happened to my father. If he is dead, I entreat you to return his body to me so that I may say farewell to him and bury him suitably.'

He gave her a long, thoughtful look before he finally spoke.

'I am afraid I do not know what has

happened to Sir Harry. I suspect he knew this castle could not be defended and is making for the coast, hoping to take ship to France.'

Anger flared in her eyes.

'My father would never run away and leave me,' she began hotly, and then stopped abruptly and bit her lip. Her father had often said that survival came first and any moral questions could be debated later. Had he acted on that principle now?

Philip Alvedon was waiting for her to continue, but as she remained silent he gestured to the men with him, indicating they should leave, and soon he stood alone with Kate while Jean, her maid, hovered in the background in attendance on her mistress.

'It may be some time before we know what has happened to your father. Meanwhile the question of your own future remains to be decided. Your father swore to uphold the laws of this country and by breaking his oath he has forfeited all his possessions. As a consequence of his behaviour, therefore, you yourself are now penniless and homeless.'

She had been too busy worrying about her father to consider her own position, vaguely assuming that after the castle's defences had been dismantled the conquerors would ride away, leaving her to manage as best she could. Appalled, she took refuge in anger.

'So what will happen to me?' she demanded. 'Am I to be turned out of my home to wander the country like a beggar?'

Mentally she was already reviewing which of Sir Harry's friends and neighbours might give her shelter, but Philip Alvedon cut those thoughts short.

'Her Majesty would not be so cruel.' He paused significantly. 'Of course, neither could she leave you at liberty for malcontents to use as a possible focus of insurrection in this restless area of her realm. That would mean more uncertainty, more fighting, more suffering for her subjects, with possible starvation if crops cannot be sown or tended. You will be kept a prisoner somewhere in England, far from the Borders.'

'So no one will care whether I live or die.'

He nodded gravely.

'It is unfortunately true that prisoners with no fortune to help them and no influential friends to intercede for them do tend to die young.'

She stared at him helplessly. It had never occurred to her that she would face prison. She had not committed a crime. But reluctantly she could see the logic of removing her from any sympathisers. There was a long pause, and then he said abruptly, as if an idea had just occurred to him, 'There is an alternative.'

She looked at him in sudden hope. He hesitated, and then said, 'You could marry me.'

Kate stared at him in confusion,

while Jean gave a little yelp of surprise.

'If you marry me, the Queen will trust me to keep you from any mischief, and as my wife you will be well cared for.'

She laughed harshly, dismissing this absurd idea. 'Is that a good reason for marriage?'

'It is as good as many I have heard. Marry me, or die.'

So he had given her the choice that was no choice. Kate stirred in her chair. Now all she could do was wait to see what would happen to her next. Meanwhile she could make herself useful and help Jean sort out her belongings.

It was an hour before a rap on the door signalled the arrival of the messenger who had demanded the surrender of the castle. His manner was subdued, and she realised with wry sympathy how difficult it must be for him to adjust to the fact that the prisoner before him was apparently about to become the wife of his lord.

'If you agree,' he said with careful politeness, 'Lord Alvedon has arranged for the marriage ceremony to be performed in an hour's time, in the castle chapel.'

'Tell my lord that I shall be ready.'

When he had gone Jean appeared beside her, her hands full of lace.

'What are you going to wear for the wedding?' she enquired, and jumped as Kate rounded on her.

'I shall wear this!' she said fiercely, indicating her black dress. 'This is not a celebration! For all I know, my father is dead, and I am going to marry the man responsible for his death!'

In the end she allowed Jean to drape a lace veil over her hair, telling her that any further attempt at bridal finery would be a mockery. When the messenger returned to lead her to the chapel the young maid followed closely, determined to miss nothing of this great event. Kate noted how the two armed guards outside her door fell in behind her as she passed. Presumably they now saw themselves as her bodyguard rather than her gaolers.

They made their way down the staircase and through the great hall. There was no obvious sign of the change of power, but she could not see the face of even one of the servants who had watched her grow up. That hurt.

Kate hesitated as they approached the chapel. Generations of her family lay buried there, but it did not look as if her father would rest in peace with his forefathers. The messenger, who had informed her grimly that he was Captain Edward Proctor, sensed her uncertainty and looked at her anxiously, afraid that the docile figure beside him was about to change her mind and upset his master's careful plans. She shook her head to reassure him that there would be no trouble and resumed her steady progress.

The chapel was virtually empty except for half-a-dozen soldiers who waited there either from duty or curiosity. Lamps gleamed only where the Earl stood with his second-in-command in attendance, and where a minister that Kate vaguely recognised as from a nearby village fidgeted anxiously near them. She felt very cold and her body seemed to be moving of its own volition without any direction from her brain.

She neared the altar, curtsied to the minister, and then Philip Alvedon took her hand. Throughout the brief ceremony she was aware that his touch seemed to burn against her freezing flesh.

When the ceremony required a wedding ring there was a pause. Obviously this detail had been overlooked. Then Philip Alvedon drew a plain gold ring from his left little finger and slid it on Kate's ring finger. It was warm from his hand and she gave an involuntary shudder.

The minister stopped speaking. Kate waited for him to continue, and then realised with shock that the ceremony was over. She had no memory even of making the right responses. Lost, she looked at the Earl for guidance. He smiled down at her formally and drew her right arm through his left, gently impelling her back into the hall where Proctor was waiting.

'If your ladyship will come with me,' the captain requested. She blinked at the unfamiliar title and then turned to the man whom she must now think of as her husband.

'Where must I go? What happens now?'

Philip Alvedon spared a few seconds to give his wife her instructions.

'I am meeting someone at Hexham this evening and I must ride hard to get there in time,' he informed her. 'This affair has delayed me. Pack what you need, but take as little as possible. Captain Proctor will escort you and your maid to Hexham tomorrow. Anything you lack can be found on our way, or when we reach London.'

He took her hand and kissed it briefly, as if it had occurred to him tardily that some gesture was expected when leaving a newly married wife. He bowed, and then his heels clicked briskly on the flagstones as he strode towards his waiting horse and away from the woman he had taken as his wife ten minutes earlier.

Proctor escorted Kate back to her rooms, where she struggled with a mixture of anger and humiliation while Jean continued packing, excited by the prospect of leaving the Borders for London. Going through her mistress's wardrobe suited the girl very well, especially when Kate gave her some clothes to outfit her for the journey. However she protested at the sombre clothes that Kate selected for herself.

'But you're a bride! You can't wear black all the time!'

Kate smiled bitterly. 'I don't see my marriage as a cause for celebration. I will be mourning for my father and my lost home.'

Jean snorted disbelievingly. 'I don't think Sir Harry is dead. It would take more than a few English soldiers to kill him.'

'I hope you are right, but until I hear he is safe I will wear black.'

'But what will the Earl say? You are a countess now. You could have splendid clothes.'

'What I wear is my concern,' Kate snapped, losing patience, and the maid took one look at her grim expression and decided to drop the subject.

Jean helped prepare her mistress for her solitary wedding night, though Kate did not sleep much, and a small cavalcade set out early the next morning. Kate rode her own horse while Jean, who had taken a hurried farewell of her family in the nearby village, was perched behind one of the troopers.

As they rode away Kate turned for one last look at the castle and saw Alvedon's men excavating the base of the outer walls preparatory to blowing them up. The castle had been her home all her life and all her memories were associated with it. Once it was out of sight she let her horse carry her along while she brooded silently. A new life was beginning, and so far its shape was completely unknown to her.

She wondered what London would be like, and whether she would meet the great Queen, Elizabeth of England. But most of all she wondered why Philip Alvedon had married her. Finally she concluded that he had taken pity on her, as a man might rescue on impulse a kitten that would otherwise be drowned. But kittens grew into cats. The Earl might find his good deed would bring him trouble in the future.

2

There were plenty of people bustling in and out of a large house near Hexham when Kate and her party arrived in the afternoon, but Philip Alvedon was not waiting to greet his bride. Captain Proctor helped her dismount and after a quick word with one of the soldiers by the doorway he led her indoors to a large room where she saw Lord Alvedon sitting at a table, dictating letters to a secretary in between answering questions from various anxious-looking enquirers. He did not see the newcomers at first and Proctor cleared his throat.

Philip Alvedon looked up, frowning, and Kate was positive that in that first instant he did not recognise her. Then he was on his feet, coming forward to take her hand and kiss it.

'My lady,' he greeted her briefly. 'I have found a travelling carriage for you and your maid which should be comfortable enough for the rest of your journey to London. Captain Proctor and a dozen men will escort you. You will spend the first night here, and I will arrange your other lodgings as I travel south ahead of you.'

Having informed her of what was planned for her, he was turning back to the table, but Kate refused to be dismissed so quickly.

'You will not be with us?' she said in pretended surprise.

'Unfortunately that is not possible. I must reach London and the Queen as soon as I can.' He paused, at last uncomfortably aware that once again he was not behaving like a new husband, and sought for something else to say. 'I will be able to have Mayburn House prepared for the arrival of its new mistress,' he managed. 'Now, a room has been put aside here for you and your maid, so you may rest.'

A second later he was already speaking to someone else and Kate had no alternative but to let herself be guided through the house by Captain Proctor up to the large well-furnished room which had been assigned her. Here, it was Jean who could contain herself no longer.

'Well!' she burst out. 'If this is what gentlemen from London call a marriage, I'm glad I'm a northerner!'

Kate collapsed in laughter which was tinged with hysteria at first, but soon became real amusement.

'Give the man a chance, Jean. Yesterday morning he hadn't even met me. He is doing his best.'

Before they could say more there was a tap on the door and a flustered middle-aged woman came in who was obviously torn between pride at having such distinguished guests and despair at the chaos it had caused in her household. She apologised several times for her poor hospitality before Kate could tell her that everything was satisfactory.

Reassured, she lingered while servants brought in refreshments, her eyes noting every detail of the new Countess of Mayburn. She was satisfying her own curiosity now, and would soon be satisfying that of her neighbours. Kate began to realise that her new social status would make a big difference to her life and the way people would treat her.

Soon after, she watched from the window as Philip Alvedon rode away without looking back and without having bothered to say farewell to her.

Next morning the travelling carriage her husband had contrived to find was waiting to convey Kate and Jean on their slow journey along the rough roads of northern England. Food and wine had been packed for their midday meal, and when shadows began to lengthen they arrived at a country house where another anxious lady was waiting to welcome her guests.

The following days followed the same pattern and soon began to blur into each other. Kate's body ached from the jolting progress of the carriage and she found it difficult to sleep at the unfamiliar houses where she ate, went to bed, and thanked her hosts politely for their hospitality. All she really wanted was a quiet room where she could be alone and rest without the prospect of another day's journey.

Captain Proctor was dour and uncommunicative, but Jean was soon on friendly terms with many of their escort and passed on the information she gleaned to Kate.

'They all agreed that Lord Alvedon is one of the richest and most powerful men in the Kingdom,' she informed her mistress. 'He owns half Derbyshire as well as land in the south. Queen Elizabeth trusts him completely, and takes his advice almost always, so the Spanish and French ambassadors are his enemies. They say,' she went on with a sideways look at her mistress, 'that he is a just man, but very strict and unforgiving.'

'And what do they think of his sudden marriage?'

'They were surprised,' Jean said diplomatically.

At last one evening Captain Proctor came to speak to her.

'We are not far from London now,' he told her. 'If you wish, we can make a shortish journey tomorrow and then reach London the following day. Alternatively, we can start very early tomorrow and travel on till we reach London, though we will not get there before nightfall. Which would your ladyship prefer?'

Kate did not hesitate. 'I am tired of travelling. Let us get to London tomorrow.'

In fact Kate and Jean were settled in the carriage when dawn had just begun to break and the day seemed unending. Then, as the sun was setting and Kate was almost asleep with exhaustion, Philip Alvedon and horsemen carrying torches met the carriage and escorted it to Mayburn House, the great mansion beside the Thames. The carriage finally halted outside the imposing doorway and its master handed his new countess down from the carriage and led her into the building.

She was conscious of the blaze of lights from hundreds of wax candles and saw two rows of servants drawn up to greet her. With a great effort, she held her head high as she was led through their ranks, aware of their eager, speculative expressions as they watched her pass. She smiled mechanically at some of them who bowed or curtsied as they were presented, but was thankful when the tall, dignified housekeeper led her to her rooms. Kate stayed awake just long enough for Jean to help her undress and then she gratefully sank into the waiting bed and fell asleep.

She was completely unaware that an hour later Philip Alvedon came quietly into the room and stood by the bed, gazing down at her by the light of the fire that still glowed in the hearth. His expression was unreadable. Kate stirred and turned, muttering something in her sleep. He waited till she was still again, then gently pulled the covers up round her and left as quietly as he had come.

When she woke the next morning and lay looking at the room, her eyes widened at the unaccustomed luxury of carved wood and silken hangings. Jean appeared with a pitcher of hot water soon after she rang the bell by the bedside and the maid was obviously overawed by her new surroundings.

'I have a room all to myself!' she said, wide-eyed. 'And you should see the servants' hall, mistress — I mean, my lady.'

After Kate had made her toilet and Jean had helped her to dress, the housekeeper came, escorting a servant with a loaded tray.

'His lordship asked me to apologise to you for his absence this morning, but he has been summoned to the palace. He told me you would probably prefer to breakfast in your room,' she said, and directed the servant to place the tray on a table near the large window. 'Perhaps later you will inspect your rooms here and tell me if you would like anything changed.'

Kate, nearly as overawed as Jean by the housekeeper's impressive dignity, thanked her and, as the woman stood waiting with folded hands for any requests, looked round her bedroom for something to comment on. Jean and the housekeeper had come in by a door which evidently led to the rest of Kate's suite of rooms. Another door, as Kate had discovered already, led to a dressing-room. There was yet another small door, however, and Kate pointed to it.

'Where does that lead?' she asked.

There was silence in the room, then a smothered giggle from Jean.

'That door,' replied the housekeeper, 'leads to his lordship's bedroom.'

Kate lingered in her rooms until she decided she could no longer delay venturing out into the rest of the great house of which she was now nominally the mistress. Then she was disconcerted to discover that a servant was stationed permanently outside her rooms to listen for her bell so that he could run her errands and summon anyone her ladyship wished to see.

When she announced that she was preparing to explore the house he fetched the steward, who was even more imposing than the housekeeper and who insisted on conducting her on an exhaustive tour of the principal rooms. She felt like a visitor awed by the splendour and could not imagine how she could ever come to regard Mayburn House as her home.

Philip Alvedon appeared in the afternoon and the servants discreetly removed themselves. Left alone together, the couple's conversation was formal, consisting mainly of his enquiries about her accommodation and whether she had recovered from her journey, and Kate's brief replies.

At dinner, servants far outnumbered the two who sat in virtual silence except when Philip roused himself to make some remark. At the end, he suggested that she might wish to retire early, as she must still be tired from her long journey. Was he going to spend all their married life suggesting that she needed to rest?

Kate obediently withdrew to her rooms where she sat for an hour, wondering how much of the rest of her life she would spend alone there. Then she stirred herself and sent the servant at the door for Jean, who prepared her for bed.

That night Philip Alvedon came through the small door, wrapped in a loose gown of rich eastern brocade, and she found herself wondering why a man who dressed so soberly by day should choose such display in his private hours.

He stood by her bedside and held out a piece of paper.

'This was intercepted two days ago.'

She looked at it carefully, and then with a jolt she recognised the scrawl that covered the paper. It was from her father, and was very short.

Daughter, I have heard that you are safe. I hope to get to France and will send you news when I can.

That was all.

'Thank you for bringing me this,' she said gratefully.

Philip Alvedon shrugged. 'How could I sleep with a woman who thought I had killed her father?' he asked. Then he snuffed out the candle by the bed and let the rich robe fall to the floor.

Later, he slid from between the sheets, gathered up his robe, and returned to his own room without a word while she stared into the darkness. The marriage ceremony, the ring on her finger, had had little significance, but now she belonged to Philip Alvedon.

Jean seemed unusually slow and clumsy the next morning, and when Kate snapped at her impatiently she burst into tears. Kate took her in her arms till the girl stopped crying.

'What's the matter, Jean?'

'I want to go home!'

Kate's heart sank. If Jean left her there would be no link with her former life left, no-one with whom she could talk about Northumberland.

'It's only natural to be a little homesick at first,' she said soothingly, 'but that will soon pass. Remember, we haven't seen the sights of London yet.'

'I don't care!'

Further questioning revealed that some of the servants had been sneering at the girl's country origins and inexperience, teasing and mocking her until she dreaded going to the servants' hall.

'They say you should have a proper maid, not a country girl like me!'

Kate's lips tightened.

'That's nonsense. You and I came south together and we are going to stay together. Don't let these idiots upset you.'

When Jean had gone, still sniffing a little, Kate sent for the steward and the housekeeper. The stately pair arrived together to be confronted by a very dignified mistress.

'I am sure you will be as distressed as I am to find that my maid has been made miserable by a group of fools who feel superior simply because they were born in London. Her welfare is your responsibility. You will, of course, speak to the servants concerned and I do not expect to hear that she has had any more problems from now on.'

Taken aback, they assured her that they would take care that Jean did not suffer any more harassment. Then the steward made a big mistake.

'It is unfortunate that the girl has been badly treated, but perhaps there is something in what the other servants have been saying. She is scarcely suited to be the personal maid of a countess.'

He stopped abruptly as he saw the look on Kate's face.

'Jean is my maid, and she is also my friend. She will remain with me,' she told him freezingly.

The pair apologised and retreated and the servants began to revise their opinion of Kate. Perhaps she was not the quiet, colourless figure they had assumed at first sight.

That evening when Philip Alvedon asked her politely how her day had been, she put down her knife and folded her hands in her lap.

'I want to know what I am supposed to do.'

He looked at her blankly.

'What is my function?' she said patiently.

He was obviously still at a loss.

'What did you do in Northumberland?'

'I ran my father's household — I looked after the servants, organised the provisioning, dealt with the tenant farmers when my father was away. Here you have a very efficient staff that deals with such matters. I don't think they would be very happy if I interfered with their duties just for the sake of having something to do.'

Pictures of his steward and housekeeper displeased obviously rose to

Philip Alvedon's mind.

'No, indeed not,' he said hastily, and she was amused to realise that there were some figures who overawed even the mighty Earl of Mayburn.

'What did your mother do?' she enquired.

'My mother died when I was born,' he replied simply and she was embarrassed, realising how little she knew about him.

The Earl was frowning, thinking about the problem.

'I believe many ladies amuse themselves with sewing,' he said cautiously. 'Others play games or practice their music.'

He looked at her hopefully but she shook her head.

'I hate sewing and this house does not need any more embroidered chair covers,' she said firmly. 'I am not musical and I don't see the point of playing silly games.'

But Philip had thought of a solution.

'The Queen is leaving to visit Oxford

for a few days, but when she returns you will be presented to her, of course. Once at court, I am sure you will soon make friends who will involve you in their activities. Presumably you can occupy yourself here in the meantime?' Philip Alvedon said, satisfied that he had solved the problem. Clearly it did not occur to him that he might help to entertain his wife.

Kate smiled resignedly.

'I still have much to learn about the house.'

'Of course.'

He looked at her critically. She was wearing one of the plain, practical dark gowns she had brought with her.

'You will, of course, require clothes suitable for court. I will instruct someone to attend you.'

Now she knew her father was alive and well she had no reason to cling to her sombre clothes, and was very well aware how unsuitable they would be for the royal court. The next day Mistress Roberts, a thin scrap of a woman dressed in serviceable plain brown, but with surprisingly shrewd eyes, duly appeared. She was accompanied by underlings staggering under the weight of bales of rich fabrics and miniature copies of elaborate gowns.

Her father had not had to worry about money, but Sir Harry had not been overly concerned about the appearance of where he lived. His castle rooms were filled with furniture that was there because it had always been there. Hangings were replaced when they wore out for the sake of comfort, not appearance. The idea of acquiring furniture, hangings and ornaments with the deliberate intention of creating a harmonious whole would have seemed strange to him.

Then her husband came home one day with the news that the Queen had decided she would see the new countess the following day.

'Tomorrow?' Her eyes widened. She was finally going to come face to face with the great Queen Elizabeth who had led England for so long.

The next day, Kate was ready in one of her new dresses.

'You look beautiful, my lady,' Jean assured her.

Kate saw the other women look past her and sink down in deep curtseys.

Lord Alvedon was standing in the doorway, his eyes fixed on his wife. As the other women rose he came forward, a small casket in his hand.

'I apologise for not remembering these earlier. They were my mother's.'

He took a rope of pearls from the casket and held it out. Kate bowed her head while Mistress Roberts slipped the necklace over Kate's head and arranged it. Kate's face glowed with pleasure when she looked in the mirror that Jean held out. She had never dreamed she could look like this.

'Now I can face the Queen and the court!'

3

Guided by her husband, Kate curtseyed low, her stiff silk skirt billowing around her, and waited for the Queen to speak. Her heart was beating uncomfortably fast. Queen Elizabeth had been ruling England for nearly forty years while other rulers died and ministers came and went, and while Elizabeth ruled, England felt safe. Nobody could approach her without some awe, especially a young girl who had never known another sovereign.

'Let me see your face, child,' said a surprisingly harsh voice. Kate tilted her face up obediently and the two women looked at each other. Kate had been prepared for the Queen's elaborate jewel-encrusted robes and warned about her red wig, but no women she knew in Northumberland had used cosmetics. To her Queen Elizabeth's painted face looked like a mask, apart from the bright black eyes.

The thin, painted eyebrows rose slightly, and Kate realised she had been staring too boldly and lowered her gaze.

'You are a pretty little thing,' the harsh voice commented. 'It is unfortunate that your father has seen fit to break our laws. Can you say anything in his defence?'

Kate coloured. Elizabeth knew very well that practically every gentleman on the Borders had broken the same laws as Sir Harry.

'Your Majesty, I cannot defend what he has done, but to me he was always a kind and loving father.'

An icy silence seemed to settle on the hall. A split second too late Kate realised that those within hearing suspected she was deliberately comparing her own father with Henry VIII, Elizabeth's own very unkind and unloving father. She closed her eyes in horror, and then the Queen's loud laugh broke the silence.

'So you have spirit enough to defend him! Lord Alvedon, I trust your bride will be kind and loving to you.'

She gestured to Kate.

'Rise, my lady. I hope to see you at my court again.'

Kate was grateful for Philip's steadying hold of her arm. She felt weak.

'I wasn't thinking when I spoke,' she managed to say urgently as he led her away, but he reassured her.

'She knew that, and she decided to be amused.'

'That was kind of her.'

A shadow crossed his face.

'She is growing old. It takes less energy to be amused than to be angry.'

The lights in the great hall glittered on the jewels which decorated the elaborate costumes of the dozens of courtiers, most of whom seemed anxious to inspect the new countess. Fortunately Philip Alvedon was held in healthy respect and no-one was prepared to approach him until he had indicated by a smile or a gesture that he wanted to speak to them, but Kate still lost count of the people who were presented to her, and soon gave up all attempts to remember their names.

Some, she knew, were powerful men who helped Elizabeth rule. Others were escorting young daughters whom they obviously saw as suitable companions for the Countess of Mayburn.

One couple did catch her attention. Sir Matthew Ramsay was middle-aged, short and broad, and looked as if he would have been more at home on a farm than at court, but that had not stopped him dressing himself in yellow velvet. His wife, Lady Margaret, was an imposing figure some inches taller than her husband and shared his taste for bright clothes.

Kate felt dazzled by the expanse of yellow satin and gold thread. Surprisingly, Philip greeted them warmly. Lady Margaret ignored etiquette and took Kate's hands.

'I'm not sure if Philip has realised just how difficult your new life must be,' she said directly. 'If you would like help or advice, you can call on me.'

Not everyone was so kind. She could see some ladies looking at her with disdain, or talking to friends behind their fans while they stared at Kate maliciously.

The Queen retired early and Philip looked down at his wife.

'Are you finding this first outing too much to take in all at once?' he asked quietly. When she nodded he unobtrusively gestured to one of the servants, and soon they had slipped away from the noise and the music to where their coach was waiting, with Captain Proctor and three other soldiers riding guard.

Kate sank down into the soft cushions with a sigh of relief.

'I've never seen so many people all at once!' she said with feeling as the carriage rattled over the cobbled streets.

'If it's any consolation, I try to avoid these receptions, but naturally the Queen wished to meet my new wife, and it gave you a chance to meet people who may become your friends.'

'Lady Margaret Ramsay seemed kind.'

There was a question in her tone and Philip laughed softly.

'Sir Matthew Ramsay is of humble origins. Like Sir Francis Drake, he was a privateer and he enjoys the trappings of wealth now he is rich enough to afford them. He has intelligence and common sense, and I trust him, as well as his wife.'

Kate thought back over the evening.

'Thank you for looking after me and helping make sure I didn't make too many mistakes,' she said a little shyly.

Philip reached out and took her hand and held it till they reached Mayburn House. That night, for the first time, he held Kate in his arms till she fell asleep.

As he had predicted, life did grow more interesting after her court debut. She grew acquainted with other young noblewomen and joined in their pursuits, though she sometimes grew bored with the gossip about people she did not know and the endless discussions about dress and eligible young gentlemen. However, she was delighted with one new acquaintance.

John Brand was young, handsome and debonair. He appeared one morning when Kate was sitting with a group of young ladies, and was soon introduced to her. He was elegant and amusing and had persisted in engaging her in conversation, producing a stream of comments and stories and ignoring her brief replies and downcast eyes until she had been forced to smile and then to laugh.

From then on he often appeared at the social gatherings which she attended, though she was never sure whether it was by chance or on purpose. He was the complete opposite of the Earl of Mayburn, and she noticed that if Philip was with her John Brand would wait until he had been called away from her side yet again by someone who wanted to consult him on some matter of state, and then John would be there to offer amusing company, removing himself with elegant speed when he saw the Earl returning. His conversation had moved gradually from casual banter to extravagant compliments.

'Your skin is white as ivory but glowing like a pearl. Now you blush, and your skin becomes rose petals,' had been a recent example.

She could not take such tributes seriously, but enjoyed receiving them, taking them as part of the elaborate social game the younger courtiers played.

Unused to such a charmer, because of her inexperience she failed to see how often he managed to position himself between her and the rest of the company, seeming to isolate them, and she could not see the looks being cast at them by other courtiers, or hear the comments being murmured. Finally at least one lady decided that she should be made aware of how the situation looked to the rest of the court world.

Kate was mildly surprised to receive an invitation from Lady Margaret Ramsay to join her on a boat trip on the Thames as she had only exchanged a few polite words with the lady since her introduction at court. She was even more surprised to find that she was Lady Margaret's only guest.

'I thought a quiet outing would be more enjoyable,' she was told as she was guided on to the boat and settled on to comfortable cushions by the two servants who accompanied them before six powerful rowers started to propel the boat upstream.

Soon they were passing smoothly through the market gardens that helped feed London, and then through fields where occasionally farmers looked up from their labours to wave at the little vessel.

Kate sighed wistfully.

'Of course, it's not like Northumberland here, and I do miss the open country and the fresh air. My lord says he will take me to Mayburn Castle when he can, but that may not be for some time.'

Lady Ramsay gave her a sideways glance.

'I know your husband must be eager to show you Mayburn. It was his childhood home, after all, and he always speaks of it with great affection.'

'But he can never find an opportunity to take me there!'

'That is not his fault!' Lady Ramsay said with asperity. 'You must know how the Queen depends on him and wants him near her.'

'She has other counsellors!'

'Very few whom she can trust like Philip Alvedon or who have his intelligence. You have to accept that he will always put his Queen and country before his own wishes, or yours.'

Kate fidgeted irritably. She was used to telling others what to do, not being spoken to like a girl still in the schoolroom. Lady Ramsay must have seen this, for she changed the discussion to more innocuous matters.

Eventually the boat was mooring by a grassy spot and the servants hurried to lay cloths on the ground and covered them with refreshments before being given permission to go and join the rowers for their own meal.

'I like being informal sometimes,' Lady Margaret informed Kate, pouring wine for them both. 'It means we can talk more easily.'

This sounded ominous, but in fact little was said before they had finished the light meal. Then Lady Ramsay wiped her mouth and hands on her napkin and sat up purposefully, and Kate realised that she was about to find out the reason for the boat trip.

'I brought you here so we can discuss your foolish behaviour with Master John Brand,' the older woman said baldly. Kate stared at her in amazement and then in fury before standing upright and regarding Lady Margaret with all the dignity she could muster.

'I am not prepared to discuss my friends with you,' she said stiffly. 'Tell your servants to have the boat launched. I want to go back to London at once.'

Lady Ramsay did not move, nor did she look worried.

'I will tell my servants when I am good and ready, and I warn you that they will only obey me. As your only way back to London is on my boat, you might as well sit down and listen.'

Kate stayed upright, seething, aware that she could not walk back to London on her own and was not ready to get embroiled in a shouting match with Lady Ramsay's servants. There was indeed no escape.

Lady Ramsay patted the cushions. 'You can stand if you like, but you'll have to listen and you will be more comfortable sitting down. If you like, I'll change 'foolish' to 'unwise'. It does sound a little better.'

Kate sat down slowly, but kept her face resolutely turned away from Lady Ramsay although she could not shut out the sound of her voice.

'Master Brand is charming, good

looking and amusing. He is also an underhanded, scheming cold-hearted wretch who has deliberately set out to ruin you.'

Kate spun round furiously, only to be silenced by Lady Margaret's look of determination.

'Do you know Lady Diane Morley?'

A memory came back to Kate of a striking woman she had seen one evening with jewels highlighting her copper-coloured hair and her bodice cut so low as to verge on the immodest.

'She is John Brand's cousin and an ally in many a nasty little affair. I suspect she has put him up to this.'

'Why should she wish me harm?'

Lady Margaret sighed impatiently.

'Lady Diane very much wanted to be the Countess of Mayburn. In fact I think she had convinced herself she would be, because she told her friends it was only a matter of time. Then Philip Alvedon went to Scotland and suddenly reappeared with a wife. All Lady Diane's hopes were dashed and she was made to look very foolish.

'In addition, various jewellers and dressmakers were happy to give her credit when they thought she was going to marry a rich man, but now they are dunning her for payment. If people believe that John Brand has seduced you she will be very pleased.'

'But I would never be unfaithful to my husband!'

The older woman patted her hand.

'I know that. But you don't have to be. If Master Brand can somehow get you alone for ten minutes, that will be enough. You can declare your innocence and he will say nothing wrong happened — but he will smile in a certain way or wink at a friend and that will be enough. Your reputation will be ruined and irretrievable harm done to your marriage.'

She spoke with convincing confidence, and Kate was forced to think back over recent encounters with John Brand. There had been times when he had tried to persuade her to go somewhere apart with him. She had refused, of course, putting the requests down to youthful thoughtlessness. Now she was near tears of mixed fury and humiliation.

'But why should they want to hurt me? I didn't ask Philip to marry me!'

'They want to take a petty revenge on you, of course, but if they harm you, they harm your husband as well. A scandal would cast doubts on his judgement, and you know how important trust is.'

She looked at Kate's slumped shoulders.

'Elizabeth's court is not a place for innocent games. Don't blame yourself. You are inexperienced.'

'I was a fool.'

'We all are when we are young. Now, let's forget Master Brand and enjoy the rest of the day.'

'Not yet. Is there anybody else who might wish me harm?'

'You married the most eligible man in England. Quite a lot of ladies don't wish you well, but Lady Diane is the only one spiteful enough to set out to hurt you. As for former mistresses, you can't have expected your husband to remain lonely at his age, but he was never a great womaniser. He never had the time for many affairs.'

'He hasn't got much time for me,' Kate said a little sadly.

Lady Margaret had promised her husband she would not ask Kate how her unlikely marriage to Philip had come about, but she could still give advice.

'Philip Alvedon has always been a lonely, self-sufficient man, but he did marry you, and it must have been for some good reason. You can't go on ignoring the world we live in forever. The only thing that is of use to women like us is power, and we can only get that through our husbands. You are a good-looking girl. Make Philip Alvedon care for you if he doesn't already.'

Kate was very quiet on the journey back. Lady Margaret had given her a lot to think about. Her first concern was how to deal suitably with Master Brand.

She next saw him at a court reception to welcome a new ambassador. For some reason Philip stayed by his wife's side for most of the evening and it was getting late before he was summoned away for a word with the Queen. He went with obvious reluctance, and Kate soon found that Master Brand was by her side and that Lady Diane Morley was watching them. As usual, the young man was full of extravagant compliments, and Kate forced herself to smile and laugh as usual.

'It is a beautiful night,' he commented. 'Do you know the constellations of the stars, Lady Katherine? They are very clear tonight. Let me show you.'

He was guiding her towards a door that led to the garden. Evidently he had decided that he had found a good opportunity to compromise her in front of this distinguished gathering. She allowed him to lead her towards the door, but her eyes were searching the crowd.

Suddenly she saw the pair she wanted and her face lit up. Lady Frances Doulton and her sister, Lady Agnes, were mature ladies who prided themselves on their knowledge of scientific matters, and would lecture on many subjects without hesitation or indeed invitation.

'Lady Frances! Lady Agnes!' Kate raised her voice. 'Master Brand is going to show me the constellations. Won't you join us?'

As she had expected, the sisters bristled.

'Master Brand? I am sure we know more than he does!'

They swept forward, determined to impart their superior knowledge and John Brand looked at them with horror.

Next Kate spied Lord Anthony Spence, a gangly adolescent standing by himself.

She flashed him a dazzling smile.

'Lord Anthony! Won't you join us?'

He came forward, grateful that someone thought him worth attention. Was there anyone else? Then she saw Lady Margaret Ramsay watching the little scene and beckoned firmly to her.

'Lady Margaret! I'm sure you won't want to miss this.'

A minute before, Master John Brand had thought he was enticing Kate to her destruction. Now he found himself committed to discussing the stars above with several people, none of them inclined to let him off easily. Mentally cursing the young countess, he reluctantly led the way into the garden, Kate carefully ushering the others after him. Then she stepped back and closed the door. She would have loved to hear Master Brand suffer, but she would ask Lady Margaret for details later.

Looking round, she saw Lady Diane Morley, her face contorted with fury. Others had apparently also been watching Kate and John Brand and listening to their dialogue, and now they were openly laughing at the trick she had played on him.

She looked round further, and saw her husband standing a few feet away from her. His face was inscrutable. Instinctively her chin rose, but he smiled at her benignly and held out his hand.

'Madam, will you dance?'

They moved slowly through the stately moves of the pavane, displaying themselves to the court as a good-looking couple who were apparently enjoying each other's company.

Half-an-hour later the small group who had gone star watching spilled back into the room.

Lady Frances and Lady Agnes were lecturing a crimson-faced John Brand and Lord Anthony also seemed to be contributing. Lady Margaret Ramsay made for Kate and drew her aside, a wide smile on her face.

'Oh, that was cruel! I actually felt a little sorry for Master Brand. As soon as he started talking it became obvious that he knew nothing about the stars and the learned ladies took over. And apparently Lord Anthony knows quite a bit too. They humiliated that nasty little man! I couldn't stop myself laughing aloud sometimes.' She tapped Kate's arm with her fan. 'He knows you deliberately made him look a fool. You won't have any more trouble with him.'

'I am in your debt,' Kate said sincerely, but the lady brushed her thanks aside.

'I just pointed certain facts out to you. You planned your own revenge.'

Philip approached to claim his wife, and Lady Margaret turned to him.

'Don't you think you've got a very intelligent wife, Lord Alvedon?'

'I've known that since I met her. It is one of the reasons I admire her so much.'

Others heard him and nodded approvingly. Kate realised with surprise that she had gone in one evening from foolish victim to clever manipulator in the eyes of the court.

4

Kate was silent on the homeward journey, thinking over what had happened. At Mayburn House the steward was ready to serve them with a nightcap of mulled wine before he left the couple alone together. Kate sat on a couch and sipped her drink thoughtfully, eyeing her husband. Suddenly she put her silver goblet down and squared her shoulders.

'What would you have done if I had gone outside alone with John Brand?' she challenged.

Philip looked at her, startled, and then matched her directness.

'I would have followed you, casually, as if I had suddenly developed an interest in the stars,' he said, and his voice hardened. 'Then I would have made it clear to Master Brand that he was not to approach my wife again.'

She said nothing, and he shrugged uneasily.

'I would have protected you.'

She picked up her goblet, took another sip, put it down again.

'Why didn't you speak to me about him earlier when he first began to pay attention to me?'

He frowned and replied carefully.

'I didn't know what was happening at first. I was too busy. Then I thought it was just a harmless friendship. I saw that you enjoyed his company, that he amused you. I can't do that. But people began to drop hints and tell me more about him and what he has done in the past. I hoped he would not dare to plan mischief against my wife, but then I realised that your inexperience made you vulnerable and I knew I would have to protect you.'

He smiled suddenly. 'I didn't realise how little you needed protecting! Master Brand would probably have preferred to face me in a duel rather than be so humiliated in front of all the court!'

Kate bit her lip.

'I was a fool to be taken in by him, but you must believe that it was due to my inexperience and not to stupidity. It took Lady Margaret to make me realise what he intended. I thought he was just like one of the neighbouring gentry's sons in Northumberland. When the young people met there was always good-natured flirting between us. Nobody took it seriously. It was just fun.' She looked at Philip from under her lashes. 'Didn't you use to do the same? Flirt, I mean.'

He sat down beside her and shook his head ruefully.

'As soon as I was able to think and reason, my father made it clear that my purpose in life was to follow him in the service of the Queen. My childhood and youth were spent training me for that purpose. Both my mind and body had to be fit to serve Elizabeth. There was no time for flirting or fun.'

'But when you were old enough there was time for women?'

This time she succeeded in shocking him.

'Madam! A lady does not ask her husband such a question!'

She did not reply but looked at him interrogatively.

'All right! I learned about women. My father considered it part of my education. But there was never anyone important to me, if that is what you want to know. Now, have you any more questions?'

'Just one, which I have been wanting to ask you for some time. Why did you marry me?'

He stared at her in amazement, and then she saw a shade of defensiveness in his look.

'I told you why when I married you.'

'Since I came to London I have learned more about how women who are trapped in a similar situation are treated. I wouldn't have been a prisoner. I would probably have been put in some lowly position in a nobleman's household — little better than a servant, but not in peril of death.'

'I took pity on you.'

'All you had to do was use your power to ensure that I would be placed with a family that would treat me well. You didn't have to marry me.'

Philip gave a harsh sigh.

'All right. I will tell you the truth. When I walked into your room I saw you standing there. You were tall and slender, defiant, doing your best to look brave while your eyes showed your fear.'

'And you took pity on me?'

'I wanted to seduce you!'

She was struck dumb and he went on hurriedly. 'I'm not talking about romance, about love at first sight. I wanted to possess you but I had no time to woo you, to try to become a friend instead of an enemy. What else could I have done? I admit that for once I used my power selfishly, to get what I wanted.'

'You blackmailed me into marrying you!'

'I suppose so — in a way,' he

admitted reluctantly.

Kate lowered her gaze so that he could not see her eyes.

'Have you regretted your impulse?'

'No!' he said without hesitation. 'There have been complications I did not foresee, but my rather dull personal life has become a lot more interesting. Haven't you benefited as well?'

'You mean life as the Countess of Mayburn is better than becoming a kind of superior servant? I suppose so.'

His head jerked up in wounded pride, and then he saw the mischief in her smile and flung up a hand as if acknowledging a hit by a fencing opponent.

Kate stood up and stretched out her hand to her husband.

* * *

Life definitely improved after that night. Kate felt as if she had passed some kind of test and was now accepted by court society. Her husband was seen with her more often, and he and Lady Margaret Ramsay introduced her to a wider range of acquaintances. Instead of spending her time exclusively with other young women, she met some of the intellectuals and politicians with whom Philip spent so much of his time.

The Earl and Countess of Mayburn began to entertain at their great London house. Kate had been very apprehensive at first, but the highly trained servants were delighted to have the opportunity to show off their skills, and they and their young mistress began to work together with a better understanding of each other. Philip complimented her on her success as a hostess. She was playing her part as his wife very satisfactorily.

Of course not everything went smoothly all of the time. After years of running her father's castle, Kate did not take kindly to being dictated to by her husband or members of their household, but common sense usually prevailed.

Philip, who had been accustomed to instant obedience from everyone around him, did not enjoy having to explain why he had issued some order, but learned that his wife responded best to being treated as an equal, a process that took some time, just as it took Kate time to appreciate just how great was his dedication to Queen Elizabeth.

'I respect her for what she is and what she has done for her country,' he explained. 'Anne Boleyn, her mother, was executed when she was a small child and until she came to the throne at the age of twenty-five her life and liberty were in constant danger. She is brave and intelligent, however, and she has not only held England together in the face of threats of invasion by foreign troops, but has helped it grow in power and wealth.'

'She had Mary, Queen of Scots, executed.'

'The Queen of Scots was plotting against her, and when it is necessary Elizabeth can be completely ruthless.

She has a clear, cold brain which controls her emotions as a woman. She loved the Earl of Essex as if he had been her son, but she signed his death warrant when he threatened the peace of England.'

Kate thought for a while.

'She is an old woman now, and when she dies James of Scotland will take her place. What do you think will happen to you then?'

'I don't know. James has his following of Scots lords who will hope to gain in money and position when their king comes to rule England, and James himself cannot love the men who were responsible for his mother's death. However, apparently he is an unattractive, but intelligent man who must know he will need the knowledge and experience of those who have helped Elizabeth. Whether he thinks he will need mine remains to be seen.'

Kate asked her next question almost reluctantly.

'What will you do if he doesn't want

you as a councillor?'

She was surprised by his laugh.

'Kate, do you think I will spend the rest of my life as an embittered man with no purpose in life?'

As this was exactly what she had wondered she stayed wisely silent and he continued.

'I realised long ago that when the Queen died I would still be a comparatively young man and that her successor might not want me near him, but the prospect has never worried me. I will have done my duty to my sovereign and my country and will be free to do what I really want, which is to spend my days at Mayburn Castle and live as a country gentleman.'

Kate thought of her father and his friends and how unlike her husband they were.

'Are you sure? Do you really want to spend your time hunting and care only for your horses and dogs?'

'Of course not, Kate! There are other things to do. I want to make sure my tenants and the land are both well cared for and productive. Mayburn has a superb library and I shall have the leisure to read and study what I want.' He gave her a sideways glance. 'Mayburn is also a splendid home for a family.'

At that moment a servant came in with an urgent summons from the Queen and the conversation ended.

One nagging anxiety was eased when he brought her further news of her father.

'Sir Harry is safe and now living in Paris,' he informed her.

She drew a breath of relief.

'Is he well? What is he doing about money?'

'He is well, and has enough to live on. In fact,' he went on a little stiffly, 'I arranged for him to be paid an allowance.'

'Which he has accepted? Of course he has,' she went on without waiting for a reply. 'It was his own money after all.'

Philip was tactfully silent. Queen

Elizabeth, always eager to add to the Treasury, had seized Sir Harry's estates, but Philip had persuaded her to sell them to him, although at a rather high price. Ignorant of the price, Kate tended to regard her father's former property as her dowry once she learned that it now belonged to her husband.

'I don't know if I should tell you this,' Philip went on, changing the subject, 'but he seems to have formed a close relationship with the Scottish widow of a French merchant, quite a wealthy woman.'

Kate gurgled with laughter.

'That sounds like my father! He always said he preferred widows because they had money and common sense!'

Philip looked slightly shocked. The dignified Earl of Mayburn found it difficult to understand how his wife could love her father while being aware of his many failings.

Kate still found the formality of a noblewoman's life in London rather irksome. Nothing could be done on impulse, on the spur of the moment. If she wished to go somewhere she had to travel by coach, escorted by soldiers usually led by Captain Proctor, whose manner towards her was as stiff and unfriendly as it had been at their first meeting. She complained to Philip about this.

'Why does he dislike me so? He never smiles or looks pleased to see me.'

'He is the same towards everyone, I'm afraid. He has a grudge against the world because he does not think it has treated him fairly. Edward Proctor grew up expecting to inherit his rich uncle's estates and live a comfortable life as a gentleman. Instead it was discovered that his uncle was plotting against the Queen. His uncle fled the country, the Crown confiscated his estates, and Proctor has had to earn his living as a soldier. Still, he is efficient and reliable.'

Kate's maid, Jean, had soon adapted to life in London. Having tasted its varied delights and entertainments she had no wish to return to Northumberland and was rather glum at the prospect of spending time at Mayburn Castle in Derbyshire. One of the Earl's stable lads had caught her fancy and she was beginning to entertain dreams of the two of them running an inn in London.

'Don't you miss anything about Northumberland?' Kate asked her.

Jean shook her head emphatically, and then thought for a while.

'I'd like to see my family again,' she conceded. 'I want to see they are well and tell them about everything I have seen here, and I'd like them to meet Jamie. But I don't want to go back to those empty hills again.'

Kate felt very differently. She was tired of the noise and smells of London and longed to look out the window on to hills and forest, to see cloud shadows race across the land. She wanted to breathe cool fresh air again. Philip promised her that he would take her to Mayburn Castle in the spring.

'We'll go when the trees begin to blossom,' he assured her. 'It would be a difficult journey before then. You don't want to spend hours waiting for the carriage to be dug out of the mud!'

But when the apple blossom was in flower in Kent he had to tell her that Elizabeth was insisting that he stay in London.

'But you promised me that we would have left London by now!' she said stormily, near to tears.

'I know, but she needs me. She is an old woman, Kate, and she will be dead within the next two or three years, and then we will have the rest of our lives to do as we wish.'

'Unless James of Scotland decides he wants you near him! Then how many years will it be before our lives are our own?'

She threw herself angrily into a chair and Philip left the room without another word, stony-faced.

'I told you England and its Queen come before everything else for your husband,' Lady Margaret reminded her as they sat in her carriage being conveyed back from yet another event to which Philip had not been free to escort her.

'I know! But Elizabeth is setting out on one of her grand processions round the country soon, and Philip claims he still has to stay in London!'

'You know perfectly well that the French and Spanish ambassadors will be here, Kate, and he is dealing with them.'

Kate felt herself sinking into a childish sulk. 'At least your husband can get away from the city.'

'Yes,' said Lady Margaret rather grimly. 'He is free to sail the seas in a frail wooden ship and face the risk of being sunk by any enemy he encounters.'

Kate was instantly ashamed of herself. 'I'm sorry! I am being stupid.'

Lady Margaret patted her hand forgivingly. 'Everyone is stupid sometimes, my dear. At least I don't have to go with him. I was wretchedly seasick the only time he tempted me on board for a sail!'

Kate laughed, and then stopped abruptly as the carriage halted yet again in the narrow street. Impatiently she lowered the window.

'What is the matter now?' she called out.

Captain Proctor rode closer. 'A broken-down wagon is blocking our way,' he said briefly, then urged his horse forward towards the obstacle.

'I do not like that man!' Kate said forcefully, finding another outlet for her bad temper.

'Relax,' Lady Margaret instructed her. 'You don't have to like him so long as he does his job. Let him sort out the problem.'

This seemed to be more complicated than first appeared. The wagon had been carrying live chickens in a cage as part of its load. These had contrived to escape and now the swearing waggoner was trying to recapture them before too many disappeared into the bags and bundles of passers-by who saw his predicament as a marvellous opportunity for a free meal.

'We could walk faster!' fumed Kate, and Lady Margaret looked mildly shocked.

'Women of our position do not walk through the streets! Anyway,' she pointed out prosaically, 'the streets are filthy.'

'And smelly! They are like open sewers.' Kate felt ready to cry. 'I wish I was back home. I want to be in the open air and feel grass under my feet instead of cobble stones.'

Now her companion's tone grew stern.

'You are home, Kate. Remember, we married women have no choice. Our husbands decide where our homes are. Philip has a duty to the Queen and you have a duty to him. Anyway, there are plenty of parks and gardens in London.'

'You don't understand! There are always buildings in sight, and the smell of London. I feel trapped!'

At this moment the carriage began to move again and both women fell silent, but secretly Kate was determined that somehow, for a time, even if it were only for a few hours, she would escape from London to somewhere where she could breathe again.

5

Mistress Roberts was a regular visitor to Mayburn House now and her seamstresses were there even more often, sewing and altering gowns. It had proved a profitable connection for her, for not only was she well paid by Philip, but also several ladies had admired Kate's gowns and then gone to their maker. As a result, Kate's store of clothes had grown considerably and Jean finally protested mildly.

'It's taking a lot of time to look after all these clothes. Can't some of them go out, mistress? After all, you never wear those you brought from Northumberland.'

Kate knew that she allowed Jean to show a familiarity that other noble women would never have allowed, but she and Jean had grown up together in much easier-going surroundings, and she had to admit that Jean had a point.

'I haven't even seen them for a long time.'

'They are in a chest. Shall we look at them?'

When Jean raised the lid of the chest Kate smelt the herbs that the maid had tucked among the clothes to keep the moths away and the smell of lavender and hyssop grew stronger as Jean began to lift the clothes out.

By now Kate was accustomed to Mistress Robert's sophisticated creations and readily agreed that most of her old dresses could go out, so Jean put them carefully to one side, ready to be distributed later among the servants who saw their employers' cast-off clothing as one of their perquisites.

Near the bottom of the chest were miscellaneous garments that had been included in the hasty Northumberland packing and never seen since. Jean swooped on one bundle, shaking her head.

'Well, you'll certainly never need these again!'

‘Stop!’ Kate said abruptly. ‘They are a reminder of the old days — I might even wear them at Mayburn Castle — if we ever get there.’

So the bundle was dropped back into the chest, but when Jean had gone Kate went back and drew out the shirt, jerkin and breeches she had sometimes worn to ride with her father across the hills of Northumberland. She held them against herself as an idea slowly grew in her mind. Was this the way to regain freedom for a few hours?

When she finally outlined her plan to Jean it took a lot of persuasion, and even a little bribery, to persuade her maid to help her, and then Jean in turn had to persuade her young admirer, the stable lad, but eventually they both agreed they would do what Kate wanted, though both protested that it was against their better judgement.

One fine late spring day, Jean and a slim companion slipped out of a side gate of Mayburn House and made their way to a rendezvous at a yard a few hundred yards away. There the stable lad was waiting with a lively young horse already saddled. He took a startled look at Kate in her boy's clothes and admitted that she did made a convincing young man, but he was still very worried at abetting her in her plan, terrified at the idea of the Earl finding out.

'I'm supposed to be exercising him,' he said to Kate. 'Please, my lady, don't be gone for too long or I'll be in trouble.'

'Don't worry. I've ridden a horse like this a hundred times and if there is trouble I'll take care of everything,' Kate told him firmly, one foot in the stirrup. The next moment she was astride the young horse with the reins gathered in her hand. It was a thrilling experience. She had been feeling mildly off-colour and had blamed it on the polluted London air. Now she could ride out to the green fields.

With her long hair tucked up underneath her cap, she looked like any other youth out for a ride and found it surprisingly simple to make her way out of the busy city to the fields that surrounded it and fed it. Philip was away and she was sure she had hours to spare before she would have to turn back. She rode on happily but the highway leading into the city was a busy stream of carriages and riders so Kate turned off on to one of the minor roads in search of tranquillity.

The sunlight was clear and bright on the fresh green leaves and for the first time in months Kate felt alone, free from the court, servants, her husband. Looking round after a while she saw that there were two riders a little way behind her. Wanting to be free of them, she turned off on to another road, and was mildly annoyed to see that the riders did so as well, but when she took yet another turning and they did the same she began to frown.

A small niggle of unease spoilt her happiness as she remembered some of the tales she had heard of travellers who had provided rich pickings for highwaymen who waylaid the weak and unwary. She might not be carrying money, but her horse would be worth quite a bit to an unscrupulous horse-dealer.

It had been true when she told the stable boy that she was accustomed to riding the Northumberland hills, but she had neglected to tell him that her father had always insisted that if she was not with him then she had to be accompanied by some sturdy servant who could see off anybody likely to cause trouble.

Kate saw a grassy lane and took it. She sighed with relief when she looked back and found the two riders were no longer visible and her growing unease vanished, only to return a few minutes later when she saw with horror that one of the men had somehow taken a short cut. Now he and his horse were blocking her path a little distance ahead and it was obvious that he was waiting for her.

She pulled on the reins, forcing her

horse to turn, but now the other rider had reappeared behind her and was approaching fast. Her heart was thudding and she felt a thrill of fear. She herself had led them farther and farther away from the busy roads, creating a trap for herself! How would she have to pay for her folly?

Looking round in panic, she saw a gap in the hedge which lined the narrow lane. The hurdle, which should have blocked it, had been partly pulled aside and Kate pulled on the reins and went through the gap into the field beyond and then urged her horse into a canter across the meadow. She heard shouts behind her and saw the two riders fill the gap she had come through at the same time as she realised there was no other exit from the field. The men had her cornered!

Despair made her reckless. She kicked her horse until it responded by breaking into a gallop and she aimed it at a low point in the hedge, crouching down over its neck at the last second and willing the horse to rise. It just cleared the top of the bushes and almost fell into the road beyond, but as soon as it recovered she urged it on at top speed in the direction of the highway, not daring to look round in case she saw the men in close pursuit.

She was sweating with fear until she reached the highway safely and to her relief saw a travelling carriage trundling along towards London, escorted by four mounted servants. Quickly she took up a position a little behind the carriage so that she could share the protection.

She swore to herself that she would never take such risks again. Gradually, as they neared the city and the traffic grew thicker, she relaxed, but it was long past the time when she should have returned and Jean and the stable boy would be worried, so Kate decided it would now be safe to leave the shelter of the carriage and go ahead faster on her own.

As she passed the carriage she smiled at the servants and lifted her hand in a gesture of farewell, grateful for their involuntary protection. But at the same moment one of the occupants, glancing casually out of the window, saw her face clearly and gripped her companion's arm painfully.

'Bella! It's the Countess of Mayburn! Riding on her own and dressed as a man!'

Her companion peered after the slim figure.

'Are you sure? I must say, it does look like her.'

'I'm sure,' said her companion, settling back against the cushions. 'Wait till we reach the court!'

Jean and her sweetheart almost collapsed with relief when Kate finally appeared at the yard again, by which time she had recovered her composure fully.

'We thought you would be back hours before this,' Jean said reproachfully as Kate swung herself gratefully out of the stable.

'I'm sorry. It was such a beautiful day

that I forgot the time and went farther than I should.'

The stable-lad was looking at the horse closely. 'He's been sweating. It looks as if you have been racing him, my lady.'

'I enjoyed a gallop,' his mistress said casually. 'Now, Jean, let's get back into Mayburn House without anyone seeing us.'

This was achieved without any problems and Jean helped Kate to strip off her boy's clothes and resume the appearance of a fine lady. Afterwards Kate was glad to be able to sit quietly in her private room. She had enjoyed the ride until the threat posed by the two men had brought home to her the dangers of her little adventure and her hasty escape had been upsetting and tiring. As the sun grew low, she fell into a light doze.

She woke suddenly, aware of loud voices and slamming doors, things unknown in Mayburn House. Suddenly her own door was flung open without warning and Philip stormed in, dragging a tearful Jean by the wrist. He glared at Kate and she struggled upright.

'I could not believe it when I found that half the court was buzzing with the news that my wife had behaved so shamelessly, that she had gone riding through the town and country alone, without an escort, wearing men's clothes,' he said furiously. 'I interrogated this foolish girl when I got here, because I knew she must have helped you if it was true, and she has told me everything!'

Jean wailed. 'He made me tell him, mistress!'

Philip rounded on her.

'And by tonight you and your accomplice will have been soundly whipped and thrown out on the streets!' He threw the girl towards the door. 'Get out! You will never come near my wife again!'

Kate found her voice.

'Jean is my servant! I will decide what

happens to her!'

'I am your husband, the Earl of Mayburn, and I decide what happens to you and everybody else in this household!' He raged on. 'I would never have believed that you could be so sly, so underhand, as to wait till I was safely away and then embark on such a disgraceful escapade. You have behaved like a common hoyden and brought shame on yourself as well as me.'

'Don't be such a pompous fool! I went for a ride wearing clothes my father has seen me wear dozens of times.'

'If your father let you go riding alone then his judgement of how a lady should behave seems to be as poor as his morals generally.'

Kate was beyond speech. She flew at Philip and slapped his face hard and he reacted swiftly, grasping her wrist painfully before she could strike again.

There was a long moment when each waited to see what the other would do next, and in that moment the door flew open again and Lady Margaret Ramsay surged in. Philip released Kate abruptly and turned to face the newcomer.

'Madam! It is customary to wait for servants to announce your arrival.'

'I do know that,' the older woman returned crisply. 'Unfortunately all your servants seemed to be distracted.' She surveyed the two of them. 'Well, it looks as if I have interrupted a first-class quarrel.'

She crossed to Kate, who was rubbing her wrist.

'He insulted me, said I behaved shamefully, and then he hurt me,' Kate complained but got no sympathy.

'Is that all? My Harry would have saved his breath and given me a good beating if I'd been so silly.' She turned to Philip who was standing by in silent fury. 'She behaved shamefully? I suppose you made her think it was all a matter of polite behaviour. Why didn't you tell her the truth, that you were terrified she might have come to harm?'

The quarrel had lost its impetus with

her entry and now she took command of the situation.

'Sit down,' she instructed them before going to the door and beckoning to one of the servants who were lurking nearby. 'Some wine,' she ordered. 'And you had better bring some food for your master as well.'

Kate, shaken and distressed, had sunk into a chair, though Philip was guarding the remnants of his pride by continuing to stand. Lady Ramsay sat herself between them and after the refreshments had been hurriedly brought in, she addressed Kate.

'Now, your husband is perfectly entitled to be angry at the way I have burst in here, but I care for the two of you, and I know that for reasons best known to yourselves you don't yet understand each other completely. I don't want you to tear yourselves apart over this matter, so I suggest we discuss what happened and I will try to give an outsider's view.

'As the Earl said, the court could talk

of nothing else this afternoon but Lady Cooper's story was that she saw you riding through the country dressed as a man and showing your legs to all and sundry, with no trace of an escort. Is this true?'

Kate reddened with anger.

'I went for a ride, and I wore a jerkin and breeches, as I often did at home. That is all.'

Lady Margaret shook her head.

'Kate, you know very well that the behaviour expected of the Countess of Mayburn is very different from what is expected of a young girl. Why did you do it?'

'I wanted to be free again, to go where I wanted and breathe air which isn't full of smoke and smells! My husband promised to take me to Mayburn Castle last month, but I am still here, trapped in this filthy city!'

'You know why I could not go,' Philip began to protest, but Lady Margaret held up her hand for silence.

'You are saying you put yourself in

danger because of a petty grudge?'

'What danger? I'm here, safe,' Kate insisted, resolutely ignoring the memory of the two riders following her.

'First of all, you faced the dangers that threaten all travellers around London. There are thieves and vagabonds, landless men, who prey on defenceless travellers near the capital. Each year the bodies of their victims are found stripped and hidden. But you are the Countess of Mayburn and you risk more danger. You are not escorted everywhere you go just for show or to ward off petty thieves. There are too many people who want to kill or hurt your husband because he is of such great importance to Queen Elizabeth. If they cannot harm him, they will try to harm you instead because it will make him suffer.' She turned to Philip. 'Isn't that true?'

He nodded.

'You didn't tell me that. You should have warned me,' Kate exclaimed to him.

'I thought life was difficult enough

for you as it was. You had lost your home and had to adjust to London and the court — to our marriage. I didn't want you to be frightened all the time as well in case of possible assassins. Lady Margaret is right, I suppose. My fear for you is what made me so angry when I heard Lady Cooper's story.'

There was silence, broken by Lady Margaret. 'Well, I don't think you will attack each other now. I'll take it upon myself to pour some wine, and afterwards I will leave you to talk to each other and sort matters out between you.'

But Kate shook her head when she was offered a glass.

'No, thank you. I don't feel very well.' She rose, suddenly white-faced. 'In fact, I feel ill!' She fled towards her bedroom as the other two stood up.

'I'll see what is the matter,' Lady Margaret snapped. 'My lord, you send for her maid.'

Philip looked aghast. 'Her maid? She is in disgrace. I've told her she is to be whipped.'

'Well tell her she's needed here first!'

She hurried after Kate, leaving Philip to issue instructions that Jean was to be found immediately and sent to attend on her mistress. Then he waited. After some time he realised that he had not eaten all day and he picked at the food which had been brought abstractedly, wondering what was happening.

Finally a very timid Jean knocked reluctantly and informed him that Lady Ramsay wished him to come to his wife's bedchamber. There he found Kate lying in bed, very pale, with her eyes closed. Lady Margaret rose from a seat beside her and beckoned to Philip to come near the window.

'Is she ill?' Philip asked anxiously.

'Not exactly,' Lady Margaret replied. 'In fact I congratulate you, my lord. Your wife is with child.'

Philip looked at her in shock. 'She is going to have a baby?'

'I see the news is as much a surprise to you as it seems to be to her. I should have thought that two young healthy people, married a few months, might have considered the possibility.'

Philip was visibly struggling with mixed emotions.

'But she is ill!'

'The sickness, the slight ill-health she has been experiencing, are common in the early months. But today's disturbance has put extra stress on her. However, she's a healthy young woman. I think she will have recovered by tomorrow.'

When she had gone, Philip stood by Kate's bed, watching her. He gingerly stretched out one hand and tentatively stroked her cheek, and her eyelids flickered open and she smiled weakly.

'I wondered, but I wasn't sure,' she murmured.

'Are you happy to be bearing my child?'

It seemed a long time to him before she added, 'Yes, very happy. You will make a good father.'

She woke the next day to a world in which she had suddenly become the most important person alive. The whole household now revolved around her, and because her appetite had vanished the best efforts of the master of the kitchen were devoted to composing attractive little dishes that would tempt her to taste a few spoonfuls. When she rested no noise was allowed to disturb her. Nothing was too good for the woman who was bearing the heir to the Earl of Mayburn.

Her riding escapade was put down to the wayward impulses of a pregnant woman, though she had difficulty persuading Philip that if he could forgive her he had to pardon Jean and the stable lad also.

'It was my fault. Why should they be punished?'

'Because if anything had happened to you I would have regarded them as guilty of your murder.'

'I need Jean to look after me without any distraction, and it will break her heart if her sweetheart is sent away.'

Philip finally, grudgingly, consented to grant her wish, and Jean and her stable lad were allowed to stay in

Mayburn House after a stern warning about their future behaviour from Philip which left them white and trembling.

Even the Queen summoned Kate for a private audience, and Kate found her lying on a daybed, wrapped in a brocade robe. In this informal setting she looked like the old woman she was, but her manner was as imperious as ever.

'Sit, child!' she ordered Kate. 'I trust you are well?'

'I am better, Your Majesty. Lady Ramsay assures me some minor maladies are only to be expected.'

Elizabeth looked at her thoughtfully. 'Give Mayburn a healthy child. He has sacrificed a great deal in my service and deserves some happiness.' She looked away, her gaze unfocussed. 'I have given my whole life to my country, but I do not ask anyone else to do the same. Make Philip Mayburn happy for my sake, child. He has earned that reward at least.'

6

As the kings of Europe waited for Elizabeth to die, her councillors fought to defend her, often by deflecting pressure on to themselves. The Earl and Countess of Mayburn constantly had to postpone their departure for Mayburn Castle, but as the summer heat encouraged diseases to flourish in London, Philip reluctantly decided to send Kate to stay at a pleasant country mansion he owned in Kent, where he visited her as frequently as he could.

Philip's servants still attended on her and she was as carefully guarded as ever, but her brief involvement with court society faded and as the child grew within her she was content to settle into a quiet routine and spent most of her time in the pleasant gardens surrounding the house.

'I have insisted, however, that I shall

take you to Mayburn Castle for the birth of our child,' Philip told her during one brief visit. 'I was born there, and so was my father. I am just sorry that he did not live to greet his grandchild.'

Kate stole a look at him.

'Remember, it will be my father's grandchild as well. Do you want his blood in your heir?'

He smiled wryly at some memory.

'My father insisted that I should go with him everywhere to learn the skills of diplomacy. When I was twelve he took me with him to a meeting in York with some northern lords and gentlemen. I met your father there. To everyone else I was an awkward, gauche young lad, and they ignored me as far as possible, but your father treated me like an equal and listened to my naïve opinions as if what I said mattered.

'He was so charming that I wished he were my father. Private life did not exist for my father. I wasn't a child to him but his successor to be suitably trained.

I felt your father had betrayed me when I found later that he had broken the laws he had sworn to keep. But for the sake of his kindness to an unhappy boy, I am glad his blood will run in my child's veins.'

'I know how you felt,' Kate said softly. 'He charmed people because he wanted everyone to like him, but he was completely unscrupulous. I learnt that early on, but I still loved him. He adored my mother, but after she died he would fall in love in an instant and for a few weeks or months some poor woman would be convinced that he would love her forever. Then he would see someone new and the last mistress would be abandoned without pity.'

'And yet you still love him?'

'Deeply. He taught me that you have to acknowledge the good in people and not condemn them utterly because they have faults as well.'

'My father was the opposite. He never forgot or forgave a fault, but I could trust him completely. If he gave his word he had to keep it, or he would have felt that he had failed himself.'

'Let us hope our child will combine the better qualities of its grandfathers.'

'A charming and trustworthy son! I would like that.'

'Or a charming and trustworthy daughter. Have you thought of that?'

His serious face broke into its rare smile.

'I am aware of the possibility. And I think I would like a daughter, providing she is as beautiful as her mother.'

Colour came into her cheeks at the compliment. Philip Alvedon rarely made pretty speeches.

'Do you miss your father?' he enquired.

'Yes. I often find myself thinking of him. I wasn't a good child like you. In fact I was always getting into scrapes. My nurse would complain to my father and he would order her to send me to him to be beaten.'

Her husband looked at her in horror.

'Your father beat you?'

'He would look very stern and give me one small tap on my hand, and I would dissolve into tears and bawl so loudly that he would give me sweet-meats to make me stop, and then he'd kiss me and I'd get a treat or a present. He was such fun!'

Then she looked up impatiently as she heard a familiar heavy tread approaching.

'Captain Proctor! I cannot like that man!'

'He is a capable man who has never failed me.' Philip stood up reluctantly. 'It means it is time for me to leave. I wish we were at Mayburn, together.'

As the autumnal winds began to blow, Philip stood firm against the concern of his fellow councillors, received reluctant permission for his absence from the Queen, and announced to the world that he was taking his pregnant wife to Mayburn Castle so that their child would be born at his ancestral home.

Kate grew very impatient with the seemingly endless preparations for the journey to Derbyshire but finally she said farewell to Lady Margaret Ramsay, who promised to keep her in touch with London events, and the Earl's great travelling carriage set off, followed by another carriage carrying luggage, and surrounded by servants on horseback and guards who were led, of course, by Captain Proctor.

Rains turned the roads to mud through which the carriages lumbered, and everywhere they stopped their hosts hastened to do honour to one of the most powerful men in the country and to discuss with him their worries over what would happen when the old Queen died. Philip was polite, patient and reassuring, but it all took time.

As they travelled farther north towns grew smaller and the stretches of open country between them were wilder, but slowly they were coming closer to Derbyshire, until at last Philip could assure her that the next day they would reach their home, Mayburn Castle.

They made good progress and when

they stopped at midday for some food Captain Proctor suggested that he should ride ahead with servants and some of the soldiers so that all would be ready for the Earl and Countess when they arrived at their castle. It seemed a sensible proposal, as the riders would be able to travel much faster than the carriage.

'Shall I go with them, my lady? I can see if your rooms are as you like them,' Jean suggested, and Kate remembered that her maid's sweetheart was among the servants escorting them. Philip frowned at the idea of Kate being left without a woman to look after her, but Kate laughed at his worries.

'It will only be for a few hours! What can go wrong?'

So Jean rode off happily behind her sweetheart and the carriage continued along the narrow road between the desolate woods that clothed the hill-sides. In truth Kate was glad of a rest from the maid's chatter. Her back was aching and she was very tired of the journey, especially since the weather had turned cold and wet.

She was looking forward to a warm bed in the castle but meanwhile had to be content with snuggling down into the cushions and trying to sleep. She thought longingly of other journeys when she had ridden beside her father, light of mind and body. The child within her kicked hard and she gave an involuntary groan.

Suddenly she was jerked wide-awake by the harsh crack of pistol shots and the sound of musket fire. There were startled shouts and the screams of wounded horses. The carriage lurched. Instinctively Kate rolled her unwieldy body off the seat, pressing herself against the floor. There was a pistol shot close to the carriage and one of the windows shattered. For some minutes all Kate could make out were the sounds of a confused struggle and then the door was torn open. She looked up in fear, but it was Philip.

'Are you hurt?' he demanded urgently.

She sat up gingerly, her heart thumping.

'No, I'm safe, but . . . '

'Let me help you out.'

'She stood shivering in the cold wind until a cloak was retrieved from the carriage and wrapped round her. A few guards helped companions who swore quietly as they nursed wounds and she saw two still figures on the ground, their faces roughly covered. A coach driver was cursing steadily and she realised that one of the horses from her carriage lay dead in its traces.

'What happened? Who was it?' she asked Philip.

'An ambush,' her husband said grimly, 'but I don't know who planned it. There are plenty of wild lawless men in this region, but I did not think they would dare attack two well-guarded carriages. They must have thought it was worth taking risks for such a rich prize. We killed three of them at least, but they killed two of my men.'

He looked round at the wounded

men and then at Kate, who was now quivering with delayed shock in spite of the warm cloak. 'Meanwhile, we have to get you and the wounded to shelter as quickly as possible. I've sent two men ahead to bring Proctor and his men back to help.'

The men began to check the remaining horses, but were interrupted by the sound of a single horse approaching at full gallop. Pistols and muskets were seized and levelled, only to be lowered at a shout from the rider who almost threw himself off his mount.

'My lord, they were waiting for us on the road ahead and we couldn't reach Captain Proctor! They killed Jacob!'

Philip said nothing for a moment, but his lips drew back in a snarl.

'I don't think these men are ordinary robbers. They were waiting for us. Now we can't go back, because they will have men behind us, and we can't get aid from Mayburn because they are blocking the road ahead. To stay here is to wait to die.'

He looked round at his listening men, his glance resting on Kate as she tried to grasp the significance of what had happened.

'Can you ride, my lady?'

She nodded, biting her tongue at the thought of riding a strange horse in the fading light, hampered by her clumsy body. A short time ago she had longed to be on horseback, but not like this.

Philip was busy organising his small force. 'Cut the traces, choose the best horses and take what arms you can find, and some food if possible. Leave everything else. Tie the wounded on the horses if necessary.'

'Where do we ride?' one guard queried.

'We must strike through the forest to the hills over there. If we can get over them we can reach Mayburn Castle. It's a shorter journey than by road, but it is not easy.'

There was a thoughtful silence as his audience considered the implications of what he said. The road might be dangerous, but it was familiar. To plunge into the forest hampered by wounded men and a pregnant woman was to go into the unknown with the odds against them. But no-one ventured to disagree. It was their only hope.

Within a few minutes Kate had been helped on to a sturdy mare and the small party, now numbering fifteen, left the road for the shelter and dangers of the forest. The trees forced them to ride in single file behind the Earl, with Kate in the middle, trying to concentrate on the matter of riding so that she would ignore her fear. Her reaction to the sudden violence made her feel overwhelmingly tired, almost afraid that she would go to sleep and fall from the saddle, but then suddenly she was wide awake.

Cramp had gripped her body for an agonising second. It passed and she relaxed. It was only her muscles protesting at this untimely exercise. But a few minutes later there was another pang, and then another. She tried to ignore them. Survival depended on them reaching Mayburn as soon as possible and her body could not fail her now, because if they had to stop because of her they might all die. But the pain persisted, attacking at regular intervals. She rode on doggedly, knowing that every minute gave them a little more margin of safety. A fine rain began to fall and she turned her face up gratefully to feel the cool drops refresh her as they pierced the canopy of leaves.

But suddenly she was in such pain that she cried out. The man nearest her halted, and soon the group was clustered round her.

'Kate! What is the matter?'

She couldn't speak, gritting her teeth against the pain, and Philip stared at her in dawning horror.

'The child can't be coming! It is not due for another month yet! Are you really in labour?'

She started to deny it, but another spasm seized her.

‘Can you go any further?’ Philip almost pleaded. ‘We may be able to find some shelter.’

‘I can go on for a bit,’ Kate managed to say, hoping it was true.

They pressed on with added urgency, Philip riding by Kate now and watching her anxiously. For a time the pains seemed to abate and she sat up and managed to smile at him, but then they returned worse than ever. Just as she thought herself fated to give birth under a bush the little cavalcade reached a clearing.

It was dusk now, but they could see a small, tumbledown two-storey building surrounded by a stone wall on three sides. It was obviously the remains of an abandoned settlement, where someone had cleared the forest to start a small farm before giving up for some reason. A fire was burning outside the building. Somebody had reached its shelter before them.

Four guards approached it while the rest stayed hidden, but soon they were being beckoned forward.

'It's a couple of tinkers, travelling from place to place. And there's a woman with them!'

Kate was aware of riding into the enclosure and seeing the tinkers gaping at her. Then a massive figure approached her.

'She's in labour?' a woman's voice said. 'Well, I'll do what I can to help her. Take her up the stairs.'

Philip carried his wife up the rough outside steps of the building into an upper chamber where there was a rough bed of bracken covered by a cloak. The woman followed, holding a bundle which gave a sleepy cry when she tucked it into a nest of rags.

'My son,' she told Philip defiantly. 'And I'm Martha.'

Within the hour, with the great Earl of Mayburn helping as best he could while a tinker's woman acted as midwife, Kate gave birth to her son.

He came into the world yelling lustily, as if the Mayburn pride was offended by the undignified circumstances. The woman laughed softly as she wrapped the boy in a length of fabric hacked from Kate's cloak with a dagger.

'A lusty child, though you say he has come early. Here, take your son while I see to the lady.'

Philip held the baby with awkward gentleness. Traces of dark hair were pasted to its skull by the birth fluids and its small face was screwed up and purple. Then it stopped crying and opened its eyes. Philip knew that it could not yet focus, but for an instant it seemed that father and son looked into each other's eyes. Carefully he stroked one miniature waving hand with his forefinger.

'My son,' he murmured. 'Peter Alvedon.' It had been his father's name.

'Peter Harry Alvedon,' came a weak whisper.

He looked down at his wife, with her hair drenched with sweat and her face colourless except for her dark eyes.

'Peter Harry Alvedon,' he agreed, and a faint smile fluttered on her pale lips.

Proudly Philip bore his son to show his followers, and for a few minutes their danger was forgotten as the men clustered round their lord and greeted his son. Then, reluctantly, Philip took him back to Martha and went to see what could be done to keep them safe.

The men had posted guards at intervals round the shoulder-high stone wall, trusting that even at night any enemies would be reluctant to dash across the clearing and attempt to scramble over the obstacle.

'All we can do is try to stay safe here,' Philip decided. 'My wife must rest for a while. Captain Proctor should come looking for us if we don't arrive at the castle when he expects us.'

Some miserable hours followed until the riders they finally saw approaching were not trying to hide but were carrying torches and shouting greetings. Hurriedly the thorn bushes that had been used to block the gap in the wall were pulled aside and Captain Proctor rode in with half a dozen men behind him. He greeted Philip with relief before looking round at his small force.

'What happened, my lord? When we were halfway to Mayburn Castle we met some travellers who warned us that there were brigands in the area, so as we were safely out of the woods by then I sent the rest ahead and came back with these few men. We found the abandoned carriages — and the bodies — and then followed your trail through the wood, fearing the worst all the time.'

Philip explained what had happened, interrupted by Proctor's congratulations on the birth of his son.

'And the Countess is well?'

'She is well and resting.'

Proctor looked satisfied. 'In that case, my lord, may I suggest that you and these other men leave now for Mayburn Castle. If no-one has attacked during the night they will not do so during the day when we can see them coming and kill them before they reach the wall. Some of the men, I can see, have wounds that need attention. The men I brought are fresh and we can guard the Countess till you send a carriage or litter for her and a suitable escort.'

Philip was reluctant to leave his wife, but had to acknowledge that his personal authority might be needed at Mayburn Castle. However, in spite of Proctor's efforts to persuade them to leave, two men were too badly wounded to make the journey and two others insisted that they were fit to stay and guard Kate and her son.

Philip climbed the rough stairs to the small chamber to tell his wife what was planned. She nodded sleepily and he bent and kissed her gently before turning to look at his son, who was red, scowling and fast asleep.

'They look better after a day or so,' Martha reassured him as she stood cuddling her own fair-haired baby.

Philip stood and faced her. 'Will you stay here with my wife until I return? I shall be grateful and I will reward you.'

She grinned cheerfully, showing no sign of awe in the presence of a nobleman.

'I'll stay, not because of your gratitude, but because your wife and her child need me, though I'll take your reward with pleasure,' she said firmly. 'Now go and fetch all your servants and nurses and whatever else you think she should have. I'll see she's safe here.'

7

Kate woke to find herself in a bare stone-walled room lit by an unglazed window that had lost its shutters. For a moment she wondered where she was, then turned her head and saw a large woman sitting on a stool nursing two small bundles.

'Of course,' she said weakly, 'I had a baby.'

The woman rose and came across the floor with surprising lightness in view of her bulk.

'So you did,' she said comfortably, 'and here he is.'

She placed Peter Alvedon carefully in the crook of his mother's arm and Kate tenderly touched the little face. The baby stirred slightly, but refused to open his eyes.

'I've got milk to spare, so he's had his first meal, that's why he's so sleepy,'

Martha told her. 'He's a rare appetite. Look!' She unfolded the cloth that wrapped the baby to show his stomach, tight as a drum. He slept on soundly, his milky mouth occasionally making slight sucking motions as though he was already dreaming of his next feed. 'You should be hungry now. It's hard work, giving birth.'

The men had caught some rabbits and roasted them over a fire, and Martha had ordered them to boil some in a little water so that Kate could have some broth, which she now drank gratefully.

'You are the wife of one of the tinkers, aren't you?' Kate asked after she had thanked the woman for her care.

Martha's face twisted ruefully.

'I was with one of the tinkers, though I'm nobody's wife, but he and his friends seem to have slipped away.' She saw Kate looking at the fair-haired bundle and laughed. 'You don't have to be married to have a baby, you know.'

'So who is his father?' Kate enquired curiously and was answered with a massive shrug.

'Who knows?' A shade of defiance crept into her voice. 'I've been selling my body to any man who will give me money or food for fifteen years now. John is mine, that's enough.'

Kate digested this information, vaguely conscious that she should be feeling moral outrage, but too grateful to Martha to care what she had done in the past. She thought of how her own life had been changed. She knew there were a thousand practical things to consider but she could not think of them, and the strange conversation between the tinker and the countess carried on.

'Didn't you ever want to get married, to have a man of your own?'

'There were two I thought might stay with me, but one died of the plague and the other was killed in a stupid brawl.'

Kate lay back on her makeshift bed.

'Isn't it strange how life turns out so

differently from what you expect?'

Martha might think that Kate's life had turned out a lot better than her own, but at least the gentlewoman wasn't turning from her in disgust.

'When is my lord expected back?' Kate asked finally.

'It will soon be dark, but his men think he should have reached Mayburn Castle by now. Everything should be ready by the morning, so they hope to see him back here some time after noon tomorrow. Meanwhile that Captain Proctor is in charge.'

Kate heard the note in her voice.

'You don't like him either?'

'I don't like being treated like a piece of dirt,' Martha said flatly.

It grew dark, and someone found a lantern to light the room.

'This building must have been a little settlement with a farmyard,' Martha said idly. 'The animals would have been kept downstairs at night and their heat would have warmed up here. I wish they were there now!'

It was growing colder and there seemed to be ice in the frequent showers which beat against the walls.

Kate had found her primitive bed deeply uncomfortable and was standing rubbing her back when Martha offered to try and get them both something more to eat and drink. She opened the rough wooden door and then hesitated.

'Proctor's there. I'll wait till he's gone.'

Kate stood beside her and peered out. By the flickering light of the torches that had been set up they both saw Captain Proctor approach one of the sentries, one of the two fit men who had chosen to stay. They saw him fling his left arm round the man's shoulders, laughing as if at some joke, and then they saw a flash of metal as the dagger in his right hand came up and cut the guard's throat.

At the same time they heard a cry from somewhere else nearby.

There was a moment of shocked disbelief, but Martha reacted more quickly. She slammed the door shut and seized Kate, pushing her towards the primitive window.

'He is killing your husband's loyal men! Now he'll come for you! If I help you out of the window you will be outside the compound and then you'll be able to run into the forest and hide somewhere. I'll try to delay them for a bit.'

'My child!'

'I'll pass him to you.'

Kate scrambled over the sill and Martha clutched her wrists until she could safely drop the few feet to the ground and then she picked up the newborn child in its wrappings and dropped it gently into its waiting mother's arms.

Without another word Kate, Countess of Mayburn, barefoot and wearing only her white linen shift, clutched him to her and ran into the woods.

Martha snatched up a log from the firewood and turned to face the door just as it was thrust open and Proctor stood in the opening, sword in hand. His gaze swept the room and came back to Martha.

'Where are they? The countess and her brat?'

Martha was silent, and then he strode to the window, looked out and swore bitterly before making for the door.

'The woman's run into the woods with the child!' he shouted to his men. 'Get after them! Spread out and make sure you find them!'

Martha could hear cries of surprise and saw flickering lights as the men picked up whatever they could find as torches and ran out in pursuit of Kate. Proctor turned back to Martha threateningly.

'Meanwhile, I'll deal with you.'

He strode towards her, sword raised, but she brought out the thick stick from behind her back and warded off the blow. Before he could raise his weapon again she stepped forward quickly and hit him hard on the head. There was a sickening crack and he fell to the ground. She seized his sword and dagger, then pulled him to the doorway by one leg, unceremoniously tumbled him down the stairs and shut the door. Then she sat on a stool, holding the sword in one hand with her child cradled in the crook of her other arm, and waited to see what would happen next.

After some time she heard voices as men straggled back to the enclosure. With her ear pressed to the door she managed to gather that they had failed to find Kate. There was a sudden outcry as they found Proctor's body.

'What can we do now?' one man shouted desperately, before the bellow of another man, Proctor's sergeant, subdued him.

'We go on looking for the countess and her child. Remember, we were promised payment if they died, more if we killed the Earl. We don't need Proctor. We know who he was dealing with.'

'What about the woman up there?'

said the first man. 'Do we let her get away with killing Proctor?'

The dominant voice was heard again. 'She's not important. How many times do I have to tell you that it's the Countess we are after? When we've found her we'll come back and deal with that harlot. We'll set fire to the rafters under the floor and burn her alive.'

Martha shuddered, but then the voices faded as they set out into the woods again, leaving her to maintain her vigil and hope that somehow they would not find Kate. She lost track of time, but saw that the sky was beginning to lighten gradually, and knew that dawn was coming and that Kate would inevitably be found when there was daylight to help the searchers.

Meanwhile the men were straggling back again, demanding food and drink to warm them before they went searching again. Then above their voices she heard the sound of horses' hooves and the clank of armour coming from a distance and drawing nearer and she grasped the sword more tightly. If these were allies of Proctor then there was no hope left.

But to her relief there were yells and the sound of pistols and the clash of arms. The noise seemed to disturb John, who gave a little whimper, and she cradled him to her, crooning gently. There was the sound of hurried footsteps on the stairs, and then a voice calling out desperately, 'Kate! Martha? Are you there?'

Martha recognised the voice, but did not move when the door was pushed wide and Philip Alvedon burst in, halting abruptly when he saw her. He saw the emptiness around her and his face worked, but before he could say anything another man thrust his way past the Earl and confronted Martha.

'Where's Kate? Where's my daughter?' he demanded.

'Where is she?' breathed Philip desperately.

Martha swung round and pointed

out of the window at the forest, almost veiled in sleety rain.

'She's out there somewhere, alive or dead,' she said huskily, 'and she has the child with her.'

The two men were gone instantly, shouting orders to the horsemen who had accompanied them and soon a careful search was spreading out from the enclosure. The men called out at intervals and listened for a response before going on, but the woman they were looking for was beyond speech.

It was Peter Alvedon, a few hours old, who felt the stirrings of hunger and cold, and it was his lusty cries that led them to the hiding place beneath a fallen tree where he was cradled in his unconscious mother's arms.

She was carried into the upper room of the building where Martha sighed with relief when she found a heartbeat and then set about chafing the ice-cold limbs while ordering Philip's men to find more wood for the fire.

Sir Harry Salter was upbraiding

Philip as they both watched anxiously.

'You left her in the care of a murderer! You must have known he was a villain!'

'Proctor served me well for five years,' Philip said crisply, without taking his eyes off Kate. 'I don't know yet what turned him. None of his men were taken alive.'

Kate stirred and moaned, and both men forgot their quarrel.

'We need to get her somewhere better than this,' Martha told them.

'We'll take her home to Mayburn Castle. My men are rigging up a litter.'

The litter was rough and ready, but it would serve. Kate was wrapped in several cloaks and placed on it tenderly, and then Philip turned to where Martha stood watching, the two children in her arms, waiting for someone to take the Earl's son. He thanked her first for what she had done for Kate.

'I shall be grateful if you will go on helping us and come with us now to Mayburn Castle. She should have a woman with her on the journey, and you have shown how capable you are. However, if you have other plans, if you intend to join friends in the neighbourhood, I can give you some gold and have you taken to the nearest town if you like.'

'Well now,' Martha rumbled. 'I've no friends to go to, and if I turn up in a town with gold I won't keep it for long. It will likely be stolen from me, and I may be hurt in the process, or someone will accuse me of having stolen it from them and I'll end up in prison. Now, your baby needs regular feeding and, as you say, I can care for your wife. Take me with you to this castle you are talking about, feed me, and we'll talk about rewards after we get there.'

Philip was relieved that she was willing to fall in with his plans, but he felt compelled to warn her.

'The danger may not be over yet. There could be other enemies in the forest, allies of Proctor. We may be attacked again.'

Martha shrugged her vast shoulders.

'There have been times recently when I was facing slow death from hunger. There's no hope or future for me in the local towns. I'll take a chance with you.'

'Then I'll gladly take you,' he said warmly. 'And if we survive you will find me generous.'

'I'll hold you to that,' she said practically. 'Now, let's find a cloak to keep me and these two little lads warm.'

Finally the cavalcade set off with Kate in her litter and her husband riding beside her on his horse. Martha and the two babies followed on a horse whose owner walked holding its bridle to make sure the inexperienced rider did not fall off. Sir Harry Salter brought up the rear, keeping a careful watch for possible enemies. None appeared, however, and after some hours they were met by servants from Mayburn Castle bringing a wagon packed with blankets and furs, and the women and children finished the journey in comparative comfort.

Soon the great bulk of the castle loomed ahead. The forest grew almost up to the walls on one side, but then gave way to carefully cultivated fertile ground, and a small village could be seen not far away.

During Philip's frequent long absences the servants at the castle had settled into a comfortable routine. The news that the Earl and Countess of Mayburn were coming to await the birth of an heir had provoked a flurry of preparation, and they felt they had coped well. But faced with the unexpected arrival of a sick countess and a newborn marquis, together with wounded followers, their reactions were a little panic-stricken.

Rooms were aired and heated and women were waiting to tend Kate by the time the party reached the castle, but little or no thought had been given to the care of their son.

Philip was not aware of this when he finally reached his home. His first care was for Kate, and he saw her carried to the great bed of the Countess's chambers and put in the tender care of women experienced in nursing the sick.

But the steward and housekeeper were unprepared for Martha. Their reaction to the enormous woman was confused, indignant and disbelieving. With an appearance that showed only too clearly her lack of respectability and the hard time she had had during the past days, Martha faced a couple confident of their own superiority whose first instinct was to have her ejected from the castle, until they were convinced by the soldiers that the dark-haired squalling brat wrapped in dirty rags was in fact their future lord.

Martha took the initiative.

'Take me to a warm, clean room, and I'll give my little lord what he's crying for.'

Hurriedly the steward crooked an elegant finger and summoned a lackey, instructing him to take Martha and the children to a room near the Countess's bedchamber. Once there, she was left to fend for herself while the servants' hall buzzed with gossip. She fed the children, tucked them into a nest of pillows on the bed, and wondered what to do next. She was tired, hungry and dirty, and had no idea how to go about getting this situation remedied.

Help was coming. There was the sound of footsteps running towards the room, the door opened and Jean appeared.

'I'm my lady's maid,' she said breathlessly. 'I've been unpacking her clothes, so I've only just heard about you and the babes. Do you need anything?'

Martha eyed her bitterly.

'I need wrappings for the children, as well as warm water and towels. I also need food for myself. I've never been in a stone warren like this before, so I don't know where to go or who to ask. But I know that I'd never leave someone to go hungry until she had to ask for food. I call that ill-mannered.'

'They don't mean to neglect you,'

Jean excused the servants. 'They are in such disarray because of all that is going on that they don't know what to do. I'll try and get what you need.'

She hurried out, but was soon on her way back accompanied by the housekeeper whose dignity had been deeply wounded. Her voice could be heard some distance away and Philip strode out of his wife's room to command silence, but the housekeeper was determined to voice her complaint.

'Give my lord's goods to a strumpet who comes making demands without so much as a by-your-leave . . . '

'It's the woman with the babies!' Jean interrupted.

Philip's voice was like an icy whip as he addressed the housekeeper.

'The woman, Martha, is my son's nurse. You will give her what she wants without question and with all possible speed. Is that clear?'

The housekeeper stood in stunned silence but Jean spoke up eagerly.

'My lord, can I help her? I can't do

anything for my lady at the moment, but I'm the eldest of eight and I know all about babies.'

Philip nodded curtly and went back to Kate's bedside, leaving a triumphant Jean to issue orders to the housekeeper.

The hastily summoned physician had finished examining Kate and was ready to give his opinion.

'If you are asking me to swear that she will live, then I cannot do that. The strain of what she has gone through would have been too much for many women, and she is very weak from the cold. But she is young and healthy and I think you found her in time. I may be more certain tomorrow. At least there is no infection, and you have the woman who helped her give birth to thank for that.'

Philip for once felt helpless. All he could do was leave Kate to the skilled ministrations of the physician and the nurses. He left the room, and found himself urgently required to decide on several matters, but finally managed to reach the improvised nursery where he found Martha and Jean with the two children.

'In this room, you are in charge,' he told Martha, 'and whatever you want, within reason, is yours.'

She showed him Peter and John, now asleep in cradles which had been found somewhere.

'I didn't think last night that we would end up safe here,' she murmured, pulling the linen up snugly round Peter, 'but I'm glad we got through.'

She looked up at him, frowning.

'How did you get back to us so quickly? I thought you would take hours more.'

He sat down, tiredness showing in every line.

'My wife's father was here when the servants arrived, and when the rest of us failed to arrive when they thought we should, he insisted on assembling a party of horsemen and riding out to meet us. When we met, we told each other what had happened, and discovered that though Proctor had told me that he had returned because travellers had warned him that there might be danger, in fact he and the servants had not met anyone.

'Apparently he just announced to them without warning that he and some of his men were turning back. With that proof that he had lied, we all rode for the settlement as fast as we could.'

'Then I'm glad I killed him. Did you find his body?'

Philip frowned.

'There was no trace of him.'

Martha looked disgusted.

'I can't have hit him as hard as I thought. Well, at least he should be too scared to come anywhere near here again.'

8

It was late the next day before Kate became vaguely conscious. She expected to feel cold, to sense the roughness of tree bark, and she knew that some great danger threatened her. Why then did she feel so warm and comfortable? She could hear movement, the occasional murmur of quiet voices, and she felt a cool dry hand hold her wrist, a finger on her pulse. She had to know something, but could not remember what, and sank back into healing sleep.

Hours later she woke again, this time to fuller consciousness, and opened her eyes. There was an exclamation, the rustle of cloth, and then a gentle arm went round her and supported her while a cup was held to her lips. Once again she knew that she wanted to ask something and tried to speak, but though her lips moved there was no sound.

'Everything is all right,' said a soothing voice. 'You are at Mayburn Castle and your husband and child are safe as well.'

The worry went away. She slept again.

The next time she woke she was fully aware of her surroundings, but too weak to move. She remembered the freezing vigil in the forest but when her nurses saw her face contort with anxiety they spoke to her gently as if she were a sick child, assuring her again and again that everything was all right and that soon everything would be explained.

They fed her broth and washed and changed her, and afterwards she saw them stiffen and turn to sink in deep curtseys as Philip Alvedon came into the room. At a sign from him, the nurses left them alone together.

He was wearing his usual immaculate dark clothes, though his eyes still showed signs of stress of the past few days, but his expression warmed as he looked down at his wife. She was still too feeble to greet him, but he took her hand as it lay on the coverlet and lifted it gently to his lips.

'I was afraid we had reached here too late,' he said softly. 'I was afraid I would lose you.'

He shook his head, as if to get rid of some nightmare picture, and then sat by the bed, still holding her hand. She turned her head on its long neck, unspoken questions in her eyes.

'Our son is well and thriving,' he told her. 'Martha is caring for him, with help from your maid, Jean, who seems to be a better children's nurse than she is a lady's maid.'

She managed a smile, and then there was the sound of a brisk knock and the door opening again, and Martha herself surged into view with Peter held firmly in her arms. Jean followed, holding John and peering curiously at her mistress.

'I heard the nurses say you were awake,' Martha explained, 'and I knew it was no good just telling you that

Peter here was safe, that you'd want to see the little lad yourself before you'd really believe it.'

Philip gently lifted his son from her grasp and held him for a moment before laying him carefully on the bed within the crook of his mother's arm. The rags in which she had last seen him had been replaced by white embroidered linen, and a small white bonnet trimmed with lace covered his dark hair. Martha looked on with great pride.

'I said he was a grand baby, but doesn't he look fine now?'

Kate nodded agreement and both parents gazed fascinated at the child until he stirred, a frown flickered across his face, and his tiny rosebud mouth opened wide to emit a loud wail, which John was soon copying.

Both his parents were instantly alarmed, but Martha laughed.

'That means it's dinner time,' she announced, scooping him up firmly. 'These lads like plenty of milk, and they don't like waiting for it.'

She waddled out of the room and Jean bobbed a curtsey and followed her. Philip turned to Kate.

'I've got something to tell you,' he began, but one of the women who were caring for Kate had slipped quietly into the room and now gave Philip a meaningful look. He rose.

'I'll tell you later,' he promised before leaving.

The sight of Kate's next visitor, some hours later, made her struggle to sit up in surprise. Her father strode across the room and stood, hands on hips, grinning down at her.

'Hasn't anyone told you that I'm here?'

'No! Philip said he was going to tell me something. Perhaps that was it! Does he know you are here?' She managed a faint blush. 'That was a stupid thing to say!'

Sir Harry was laughing aloud.

'Did you think I'd sneaked into the castle and was hiding in corners?' He pulled up a chair. ‘No, my son-in-law persuaded Her Majesty Queen Elizabeth to grant me an amnesty, on condition I wasn’t seen too publicly. He invited me to come here and wait for the birth of my grandchild, but didn’t tell you because he wanted it to be a surprise when you found me here to welcome you.’ He paused, his face wrinkling in mild distaste. ‘Peter’s a grand little lad, but I don’t like being called a grandfather. It makes me feel old.’

He carried on, explaining how his disquiet about the party’s late arrival and his decision to take out a search party had resulted in the rescue of herself, Martha and the babies.

She nodded, half-listening, observing him carefully. He looked older than she remembered, but perhaps when she had been living with him all the time she had not noticed age creeping up on him.

‘Are you happy in Paris?’ she asked when he had finished his account, and he nodded decisively.

'I'll admit it is very different from Northumberland, and of course there are things I miss, but I have a good life there.'

'And the Scottish widow?'

He grinned.

'So you were told about her? She's a fine woman and we suit each other well.' He looked at her closely. 'What about you, Kate? Are you happy?'

She lay back thoughtfully, and then nodded slowly.

'Yes. Yes, I am. Philip is a good man, and I think he cares for me just as I am growing to care for him.' Her sudden grin was very like her father's. 'And there are a lot of advantages to being the wife of the rich and powerful Earl of Mayburn!'

In spite of his genuine pleasure at seeing his daughter again, a sickroom was not the place for Sir Harry Slater, and he soon declared that it was time for him to visit his grandson again.

'That's if that mountain of a woman

will let me in. Last time I was just tickling him a bit and she boxed my ears!'

Philip was away for the next twenty-four hours. He had to tour the neighbourhood to reassure some of the gentlemen and civic dignitaries personally that unrest would not threaten their corner of the country when Elizabeth died.

When he returned Kate was able to greet him propped up against a mound of pillows, her hair carefully arranged and her shoulders wrapped in a soft shawl. She was surprised how glad she was to see his tall figure in the doorway and told herself that it was because she was once again virtually surrounded by strangers. He congratulated her on her progress towards victory.

'I feel well, but the physician wants me to stay in bed for another week.'

'Then that is what you will do,' he informed her.

'And I have talked to my father.'

'Ah!' Philip sat down. 'That was

meant to be a pleasant surprise for you.'

'So he explained.' She looked at him mischievously. 'What do the two of you talk about when you meet?'

Philip sighed.

'The child. You. What the cook has prepared for us. We have little in common, I'm afraid. I think he may grow bored rather quickly. But I'm grateful to him. He's good in a fight, as he showed in the forest.'

He saw her smile fade as she remembered those nightmare hours when she was hiding from the men who had sought to kill her and her child.

'Have you learned any more about Proctor, about what has happened to him?' she asked.

'I have learned quite a lot from papers we found in his baggage. Obviously someone realised that he held a bitter grudge against those in authority who he considered had robbed him of the fortune that should have been his. He was bribed and promised great rewards if he succeeded in killing my family and me. He expected the men he had hired to ambush us on the road to have no problem overcoming us because we would be taken by surprise, but he came back to make sure.

'When he found we had escaped he followed us to the abandoned settlement and persuaded me and most of the loyal men to leave so that he could kill you and Peter and then kill me when I returned and rode unsuspecting into the enclosure. It was your father, and the way he revealed that Proctor had lied to me, that saved us all.'

'But who made use of him?'

Philip's lips tightened.

'I have sent messages to London. Let me just say that an ambassador and some of his retinue will return unexpectedly to their own country within the next few days.'

'So we are safe now?'

Philip took just a little too long to reply, and she gripped his hand convulsively.

'I can't say that we are completely safe,' he said frankly, 'but I can say that I have done everything possible to make us safe. We have guards here at the castle and there are informants who will let me know if they hear of any threats against us. I must admit, however, that I will be happier when Proctor is found and dealt with. Meanwhile,' and he smiled and his voice grew warmer, 'my main concern is to see you safe and well.'

'I have been told that all I need now is rest and good food,' she responded. 'If I blink or move a finger, somebody rushes to find out what I want, and the cook seems to spend all her time preparing my favourite dishes!'

He did not tell her how strict his instructions had been that every possible care should be taken of his wife, and how any whim should be satisfied, but she guessed and thanked him.

'I keep my promises,' he said steadily. 'You are my wife. I swore to protect and cherish you, and I will keep my vows.'

A small sigh escaped her and there was a touch of colour in her pale cheeks.

'And to think we met as enemies, with you in pursuit of my father!'

'You were never my enemy,' he protested. His tone lightened. 'Anyway, my men admire you so much after the courage and endurance you have shown that I have to treat you well to please them.'

A week later Kate was protesting to Philip that she was tired of being confined to bed and that she was perfectly recovered when there was a knock on the door and Martha appeared in the doorway. For once there was no baby in her arms and she looked as if she was forcing herself to go through with some unpleasant task. She advanced resolutely.

'I want to speak to the two of you together.'

Both Kate and Philip looked at her with alarm.

'Is something wrong with Peter?'

'No. I wanted to remind you that when I came here with you and the Countess, the agreement was that you would reward me when we parted company.'

Kate looked at her with amazement.

'Are you saying you want to leave us?'

Martha's expression was a travesty of a smile.

'I'm not mad. I don't want to leave safety and comfort. But what your servants are saying is right. I'm not a suitable nurse for your son. Now my lady is in a fair way to recover, my lord, you have time to look for someone better. Give me what you think is my due and I'll be off as soon as you have found a suitable nurse. I'll always be grateful for your kindness and the shelter you have given me, but I'm a harlot and your son deserves better, and the sooner the change is made the better it will be for him — and for me.'

Philip stood, his tall figure towering over the bulky woman.

'Do you want to take your son back to the streets? Do you want to face each day not knowing whether you will get food for him or have to watch him starve? Do you want him to grow up in the gutter?'

Martha flinched.

'Of course not! But how can I stay, with my past? Let me go while I can still remember how to survive out there.'

Philip put a hand on her shoulder.

'Martha, whatever you were in the past, you are now my son's nurse. You suit him, you are good for him, so go back to the nursery and look after him and John and don't talk about leaving again.' His voice softened. 'Don't be silly, Martha. You saved my wife and son and I owe you more than I can ever repay. If you try to leave I'll have my men scouring the country to bring you back, because I want you as Peter's nurse and John as his foster-brother.'

'Are you sure, my lord?'

It was Kate who replied.

'Martha, I remember that room in the forest and how you helped me give birth to Peter and then kept us both alive. I am afraid you are doomed to a life of safety and comfort, because we will never let you go.'

Philip was sure there were tears in Martha's eyes, but she blinked them away and squared her shoulders.

'Well, if I'm staying I'll go and break the good news to Jean. She was crying because she thought a new nurse would throw her out of the nursery.' She started to leave, then half-turned. 'Thank you,' she said gruffly. 'I like it here. I've got used to regular meals.'

'That's settled then,' Kate said with relief as the door closed behind Martha. 'What is the next problem? Are you planning to go back to London in the near future?'

He shook his head very firmly.

'Not yet. Winter will be closing in soon and travelling will be difficult. I'm not going to spent weeks hundreds of miles away from you and Peter.

Anyway, it has turned out that I am not badly situated here. Mayburn Castle has started to act as a halfway house between London and Edinburgh. I am fully informed of what is happening and I can send messages in either direction.

'No, I think all we have to think about for a while is ourselves and how we are going to celebrate Christmas. I'm sure the housekeeper has her plans, but once you are up and about you must see whether you agree with them.'

'I am getting up tomorrow,' Kate said with determination. 'I managed to get Jean out of the nursery long enough to air my clothes and see they are fit to wear. Then I will be able to show everyone that I know how a castle should be run.'

True to her word, she appeared fully dressed in the great rooms of the castle and began the task of establishing herself as mistress of the household. She started with the advantage of being the mother of the heir to Mayburn and was also helped by her experience in

London and the fact that she had taken full charge of the domestic life of her father's castle for years.

Philip made it very clear that all authority in that sphere now lay in his wife's hands, although she never asked her husband for support, and a disgruntled servant who tried to complain to Philip about her orders was rapidly referred back to her.

The days when she had seen her husband as a cold stranger were long gone. The experiences in the forest had broken down any barriers that might have remained if they had stayed in London with its myriad conventions and pressures that had kept them at a distance from each other. Set apart by rank and ability from most of the people who surrounded them, Philip had essentially been lonely all his life.

Now he found it very pleasant to forget statecraft from time to time and relax at home with his wife and child. She had acquired a knowledge of affairs from her time at court, and he found that he could discuss political matters intelligently with her. She in her turn came to respect his intellect and the self-denying conscientiousness with which he carried out his responsibilities.

Peter was their continual joy. He and John thrived together, even though Martha's care was unconventional. She disapproved of the tight swaddling clothes that most babies endured and left them free to wave their fat legs in the air and wriggle on the floor. Philip rapidly became accustomed to the fact that playing on the floor with two lively babies did not fatally compromise his dignity and that strict ceremony could be relaxed without the social order collapsing.

Christmas at Mayburn Castle was not the extravagant festival of Elizabeth's court, where there was always a succession of entertainments such as masques and mummers and the aged Queen danced galliards well into her old age, but the twelve days of Christmas were still celebrated with feasting carols, and the Earl and Countess ensured that the old and poor of the neighbourhood were warm and well-fed.

New Year's Day brought in the year of Our Lord 1603 with snow flurries and Kate gazed out of the window at the whirling flakes. The past year had brought danger as well as happiness and a son. What would this year bring?

9

Kate watched the horsemen leave, heads bowed low and cloaks wrapped tightly round them as they struggled against the gale. It must have been an urgent message that brought them here in this weather and then compelled them to leave the shelter of the castle and face the storm again. Philip came to join her. He looked white, his face drawn.

'Was it bad news?' she asked him.

'The Queen is not expected to live much longer. The physicians doubt if she will last till summer.' He paused and then said heavily, 'I must go to London, Kate. It has reached a point when I must speak to certain people face to face, as soon as possible.'

'When will you leave?'

'The day after tomorrow. I have given orders for everything to be made ready.'

'I'll miss you,' she said very softly,

unwilling to add to his concerns, but Philip heard and took her in his arms.

'And I'll miss you and my son every minute of every day! But I must go. I'll be back within the month, I promise you.'

He was busy all the next day, arranging for his departure, sending messages north to Scotland and south to London, doing his best to ensure that Kate would have no cause to worry while he was away. In the middle of all this his father-in-law, Sir Harry Salter, announced his intention of going to London with him. He explained why to Kate.

'Your husband is a good, upright man, Kate, and I respect him, but his way of life is not mine, and I do not wish to live in his castle as his dependant. Deep down he still sees me as a cattle-thief and I half-feel all the time that he's watching me, watching for me to break some rule or try to steal his silver. Now I can take advantage of his journey to go south with him and then take ship to France.'

'Back to the widow?'

'Unless she's found someone else while I've been away.'

He paced up and down the room restlessly.

'I have been very happy to see you settled, and to see my grandson Peter, but you do understand why I can't stay, don't you?'

She smiled mischievously.

'I understand. Philip bores you and you don't like being regarded as just a grandfather.'

He scratched his head and grinned.

'You are deliberately making it sound bad, but yes, that just about sums it up. Don't worry. I'll be back to see how the three of you are getting on, but I don't want to live here.'

'Then go with my love and tell the widow I think she is very lucky.'

She waved goodbye to her husband and father the next day and after that had to resign herself to quiet, uneventful weeks of waiting. The winter days were tedious, grey, rainy and cold, and although she enjoyed the hours spent in the nursery she missed being able to talk freely to an equal.

Sometimes, when she grew lonely in the evening, she looked fearfully out at the dark landscape and wondered what had happened to Edward Proctor. Had he survived? Would he reappear to trouble them again?

She was sitting in the nursery one afternoon with Martha when her attention drifted away from the children as she gazed out at the road through the fields and the forest and wondered how soon Philip would return.

'Want him back?' Martha's voice broke into her thoughts.

After the way they had met, it had been impossible to regard Martha as a mere servant, and Kate was accustomed to her lack of deference. She smiled at her.

'Yes. It is so comforting to have a man I can trust and rely on. I had enough uncertainty and excitement with my father. I am safe with Philip, and like it. Our marriage didn't have the best start, but I've grown to feel affection for him.'

Martha lifted a quizzical eyebrow. 'Just affection? Is that all?'

Kate blushed and refused to be drawn into any more discussion.

Finally, one day when a weak sun was finally struggling through the clouds, a servant came running to the room where she and the housekeeper were discussing the state of the household linen.

'My lady! There are horsemen approaching, and a carriage!'

By the time she had hurried down the great staircase, the gates of the castle had been thrown open to welcome its master, who swung himself off his horse, tossed his reins to a waiting groom, and strode into the great hall to seize his wife in his arms and hold her so tightly that she was lifted off the floor.

'Kate! The miles seemed endless!' He

set her on her feet and smiled down at her. 'You are as beautiful as I remembered. Is all well?'

'All is well, and your son is trying to crawl already.'

'And I have a visitor to surprise you.'

But before he could say more Kate looked past him and saw a figure entering, swathed in furs and velvets.

'Lady Ramsay!' Kate cried with genuine pleasure, and hurried forward to greet her. 'I was told there was a carriage, but I didn't know whose it was.'

Lady Margaret Ramsay shed one layer of cloaks and embraced her friend. 'I was visiting my daughter and son-in-law when the Earl arrived in a storm asking for shelter, and when he said he was on his way back to Mayburn Castle I persuaded him to bring me with him when the weather improved. I love my daughter and her husband dearly, but after a month I thought I would enjoy a change, especially one which gave me an opportunity to see you and your son.'

The somnolent air of the castle gave way to gaiety and festivity as the cooks prepared to welcome their master and his guest with the best they could offer from their depleted winter stores.

While rooms were hastily warmed for Lady Margaret and her maid and the steward gave his report to Philip on how the castle had fared during his absence, Kate had mulled wine and refreshments brought to her private room.

'You must tell me all the news of the court since I left it.'

Lady Margaret shook her head. 'There is little to tell, I'm afraid. The Queen has finally lost her appetite for music and dancing and all the pastimes of the court. Elizabeth has finally accepted that she has grown old and that even she must die. Everybody is waiting for the end and wondering what will happen to them then.'

'And Sir Matthew? Where is he?'

Lady Margaret's expression froze.

'Somewhere off the coast of Africa.

At least, that is where he is supposed to be. He left three months ago and I have not had word from him since.'

Kate could not think of any comforting platitudes. She was well aware of the dangers faced by the men who set out on to the seas in wooden cockleshells, and of how many of them vanished without trace.

'Matthew will come back,' Lady Margaret said roughly. 'He always has before. Now, take me to see this son of yours.'

While his wife talked to Lady Margaret, Philip had dealt quickly with the steward and taken the opportunity to make his way to the nursery. Kate and her friend found the Earl sprawled on the floor with the two little boys clambering gleefully over him. Martha and Jean watched approvingly.

Lady Margaret's eyebrows rose when Martha was presented as Peter's nurse. The two women looked at each other warily, and then the grand court lady smiled.

'I can see from those two little rascals that you are carrying out your duties well,' she commented, and then she was on her knees, arms stretched out to the children.

Finally the day ended with Lady Margaret settled in her quarters, the children asleep, and everyone wined and dined. At last Kate and Philip were alone in their bedchamber.

'Lady Margaret said that the court is much changed, quieter, since we left,' Kate said.

Philip sighed. 'The Queen is dying, and she knows it. She said goodbye to me, Kate. For all I know, she may be dead now. She is leaving James of Scotland a great and proud country, though she was still refusing to name him as her successor, and he is ready to come south to claim the kingdom as soon as he receives word that she is dead. He has let it be known tactfully in various ways that he appreciates what I have done in the past, but that I may not be needed so much in the future.

'However, he is relying on me to see that this part of the country accepts the change of ruler smoothly and he will be suitably grateful. I am happy with that. I have served my country to the best of my ability and now I want to be here with you and Peter.'

He drew her closer.

The next month was a happy time. Winter seemed ready to slip away at last and Kate found green shoots beginning to appear in sheltered spots in the castle gardens. When Philip came looking for her one day he found her sitting on a stone bench, her eyes closed as she lifted her face to the sun. She sensed his presence and smiled to greet him. He strolled towards her then took her by the shoulders and bent to kiss her.

'I have had messengers,' he announced solemnly. 'Elizabeth of England is dead and King James is on his way to take his place on the throne of England.'

She looked at him in shock, taken back by the quiet manner with which he had broken the momentous news.

His mouth twisted in a smile, though his eyes were grave.

'You know I accepted that it was going to happen when I saw her last. I hope she died happy, aware of all she has done for England, and I hope that the future will be a peaceful world for Peter. Where is he, by the way?'

'Listen!'

Somewhere beyond the hedges he could hear laughter.

'Martha and Lady Margaret are playing with them on the South Lawn.'

'And Jean?'

'I suspect she is somewhere with that sweetheart of hers.'

The stable-lad who had travelled north with them was now a groom.

'Is he aware that he will have to answer to me if he gets her with child?'

'No need. Martha and Lady Margaret are both keeping a strict watch on her.'

It seemed strange to be able to talk of domestic matters at such a time, but life went on even when a great queen died.

The laughter and voices drew nearer, until the women and children came into sight. An unlikely friendship had grown up between Martha and Lady Margaret, but Philip suspected that Lady Margaret's wide experience and sophistication enabled her to appreciate Martha to the full.

Both children squealed with delight when they saw Kate and Philip, and Peter insisted on planting a wet kiss of greeting on Philip's cheek.

'It's time these two went in for a rest,' Martha announced, and made off with a child under each arm. Lady Margaret sank down on the bench.

'I regret to tell you, my lord, that there is no doubt that John has a much sweeter and more biddable nature than your son. Peter is going to be a rare handful in a few years. Were you like that as a boy?'

'No,' said Philip, rather regretfully. 'I was obedient, hardworking, and very dull.'

'Lady Margaret!' Kate interrupted.

'There is news from London!'

Lady Margaret received the news of the Queen's death almost as calmly as Philip.

'God rest her soul! We all knew it must happen soon, but it is still difficult to believe that she has really gone,' she said, with tears in her eyes. 'She dedicated her life to serving England.'

Philip was holding out a folded piece of parchment.

'The messengers called at your daughter's home and she asked them to bring you this.'

Lady Margaret read the document then sighed deeply and sat absolutely still.

'What is it?' Kate demanded.

Lady Margaret started to smile. The smile grew until she burst out laughing and clapped her hands.

'It's from Matthew! He has landed in Bristol, safe and well.' She turned towards Philip urgently. 'Are you going to London? I want to go with you.'

'I am sending messengers, but they

will be travelling fast,' Philip warned her.

'The faster the better. I want to get back to my husband,' Lady Margaret said fiercely. She sprang to her feet impatiently, as though ready to leave that instant.

In fact it was nearly a week before Philip had informed the gentlemen of the area what had happened and assembled their reactions into a report to be sent to London. He entrusted it to Lady Margaret and sent her on her way south with a strong party of riders to guard her. Kate parted with her reluctantly.

'I'll miss you,' she assured her friend. 'Write to me when you can.'

'Of course, but I'll see you in London before long. King James may be grateful that the Earl of Mayburn is not already there among the crowds who'll be hoping for office and preferment, but he will want to consult him in person before long, and he will expect you to be presented to him as well.'

'Then we'll meet again in London.'

The castle gates shut behind the travellers and Philip took Kate's hand and drew her indoors.

'Do you realise that for the first time we are here at home as a family on our own, all safe and well? I know it won't last, but let us enjoy this peaceful respite.'

They spent as much time as they could in each other's company, free for the first time in their marriage to forget the rest of the world waiting outside the castle gates. This happy time lasted ten days, until one afternoon when they were in Philip's study, looking through a pile of books which had been discovered in a store room.

Two guards stood outside the door as usual, though their presence was now taken as a formality. One of the maids appeared, ready to postpone whatever she was supposed to be doing in order to indulge in a little flirtation with the two men. As a result they did not notice the soberly dressed man carrying a covered dish until he had quietly slipped past them and opened the study door.

'Here you! Wait!' shouted one of the guards, but it was too late. The door was slammed in their faces and they heard the key turn in the lock, while the maid scuttled hurriedly away.

The dish fell to the floor with a clatter and Philip and Kate looked up from the book they were studying to find Edward Proctor standing between them and the door, a levelled pistol in his hand. He grinned at them mirthlessly.

'My lord, my lady, I have come to kill you.'

Philip stepped in front of Kate to shield her. Outside there were shouts and then thuds as the guards started hurling their weight against the door.

'Don't be a fool,' Philip said urgently. 'My men will kill you.'

Proctor's grin grew wolfishly savage.

'I know, but by the time they break down the door you and your wife will be dead.'

He was clearly mad, but the pistol

did not waver. There was another thud and the door shook as his finger began to tighten. Desperately Philip threw himself at Proctor, ready to sacrifice himself if it would save Kate. The bullet hit him but his impetus was enough to send him crashing into the would-be killer just as Proctor drew a dagger and both men went reeling to the floor.

The pistol skittered across the room and Kate seized it by the barrel, prepared to use it as a club if she could reach Proctor, but the two men were fighting a desperate battle with hands, feet and teeth, and she could not find a target in the whirling tangle of limbs.

Suddenly there was an animal scream and as the door gave way and the guards charged into the room the two men collapsed and lay still, locked in each other's grasp. The guards and Kate started towards them, and stopped as one of the men moved slightly. Philip Alvedon rolled off the body of Proctor which sprawled ungainly on the floor with a dagger sticking in its throat.

Philip, bloodstained and panting, heaved himself upright and turned to Kate.

'You are safe now,' he panted, and collapsed unconscious.

The pistol ball had caught him in the left shoulder and he was losing blood rapidly. Only desperation to save Kate had enabled him to fight on while he grew weaker. Martha, who had been drawn to the scene like half the servants in the castle by the noise, shouldered her way through the crowd and dropped on her knees beside Philip. She tore his doublet and shirt open and her lips tightened.

'Get me cloths,' she ordered Kate. 'We've got to stop this bleeding.'

Sheets were torn from beds and rushed to her and soon her capable hands were tearing them and staunching the blood. She looked up and saw Kate standing by her, looking down white-faced at her husband.

'Don't worry,' Martha said curtly. 'I've tended to plenty of wounded men. He'll survive.'

At a gesture from her, guards carried Philip carefully to his bedchamber. When a surgeon hurried breathlessly into the room half-an-hour later, the bleeding had been stopped and Philip was still alive.

Kate gripped Martha's hand as the surgeon removed the pistol ball with infinite care and announced that there had been no major damage. He praised Martha's prompt actions and gave instructions for the care of the Earl. Meanwhile Proctor's body had been roughly removed from the study. A search of the corpse revealed no documents linking him with anyone else.

Philip was young and strong and received the best of care. After the first anxious night it was clear that he would live, and in a couple of days he was protesting at being kept in bed and was soon sitting in a great chair, swathed in a fur-lined robe. Kate had hardly left his side until she could see that he was well on the way to recovery.

Now she sat opposite him and they discussed Proctor.

'He came here with me several times,' Philip told her. 'He must have used his knowledge of the castle to smuggle himself into the building. Once in, there are plenty of corners where he could lurk, waiting for a chance to attack me.'

'But why should he be so desperate to kill you that he was ready to sacrifice his life?'

'The men who persuaded him to ambush us in the forest had disowned him. He had no future and he blamed me for that.' He brooded. 'Well, he chose his own road. At least he was given a Christian burial. Let us hope he can rest in peace.'

There was silence between them for some time, and then Philip began, 'Kate,' and stopped, then started again, his voice hesitant and uncertain. 'Kate, when I was fighting Proctor, and afterwards when I thought I was dying, I had one regret. I wished I had told you that I love you.'

He stopped, and Kate's eyes filled with tears. She knew the effort that little speech must have taken. The great Earl of Mayburn, the lonely man who had always prided himself on his self-sufficiency, had made himself vulnerable to her, giving his happiness into her power. She rose and bent over him, smoothed back his hair and kissed his brow.

'If you had been able to hear me that first dreadful night when I was not sure that you would live, you would have heard me say over and over again how much I loved you.'

The tension in his face relaxed. He took her hand and kissed it and she smiled down at him.

'I have something else to tell you, Philip. I am with child again.'

His delight showed in his smile.

'Are you happy about that?' he demanded, and she nodded.

'I would like another boy, a companion for Peter,' she told him.

'And then two pretty little daughters,' he said firmly.

'That would be a good idea.'

'And I don't mind what the next half-dozen are,' he said smoothly, and laughed at her expression, drawing her down to him with his good right arm.

'I love you,' he murmured. 'It was so difficult to say the first time, but now I could say it all night, over and over again.'

Kate kissed his lips.

'We love each other.'

We do hope that you have enjoyed reading this large print book.

Did you know that all of our titles are available for purchase?

We publish a wide range of high quality large print books including:
Romances, Mysteries, Classics
General Fiction
Non Fiction and Westerns

Special interest titles available in large print are:
The Little Oxford Dictionary
Music Book, Song Book
Hymn Book, Service Book

Also available from us courtesy of Oxford University Press:
Young Readers' Dictionary
(large print edition)
Young Readers' Thesaurus
(large print edition)

For further information or a free brochure, please contact us at:
Ulverscroft Large Print Books Ltd.,
The Green, Bradgate Road, Anstey,
Leicester, LE7 7FU, England.
Tel: (00 44) **0116 236 4325**
Fax: (00 44) **0116 234 0205**

Other titles in the
Linford Romance Library:

A TIME TO DANCE

Eileen Stafford

Deborah thinks that nothing exciting happens in wartime Bristol. But then the Americans arrive, preparing to fight in occupied Europe. And for Deborah, everything changes. She finds excitement when she meets Warren and falls in love. But her romantic dreams are shattered when her father sends her away to live with her aunt in Exmouth. And more heartbreak follows when she feels forced to seek refuge in London. At the end of the war — can she ever find happiness again?

HIS LITTLE GIRL

Liz Fielding

Staying alone at her brother-in-law's cottage on a stormy night, Dora finds an intruder in the house, a man called John Gannon. He's clearly a man on the run, but Dora is charmed by him — and the adorable little girl in his arms. She decides to help Gannon, a devoted father, willing to do anything to keep Sophie safe. Too bad the only thing keeping Dora safe from Gannon is his misconception that she is Richard's wife . . .